# Will Jessica Get to the Phone On Time?

"Don't you get it?" Lila demanded. "You won the Pineapple People contest! That disgusting recipe you and Mandy entered two months ago actually won the grand prize!" Lila lowered her voice to a whisper. "And do you have any idea what the grand prize is?"

"A zillion cans of pineapple?" Jessica guessed.

"A trip to Hawaii for the winner and two friends!" Lila hissed.

"Hawaii?" Jessica echoed. "Islands and volcanoes and hula dancers—that Hawaii?"

"You've got to get to a phone, Jess! You have to claim the prize by calling the magazine before eleven A.M. on December twenty-first."

"That's today!" Jessica cried. She glanced up at the clock in the hallway. "But it's only seven fifty-five—"

"Eleven, Eastern Standard Time," Lila interrupted. "That's eight, here in California. It's a different time zone."

"Are you sure?"

"Positive. You've only got five minutes, Jessica!"

The girls raced toward the pay phone in the lobby. "Guess what the consolation prize is if you don't call in time?" Lila said breathlessly as they ran. "Pineapple! Two hundred cans of pineapple!"

# SWEET VALLEY TWINS AND FRIENDS
## FRIENDS
### SUPER EDITION

# The Unicorns Go Hawaiian

Written by
Jamie Suzanne

Created by
FRANCINE PASCAL

A BANTAM SKYLARK BOOK
NEW YORK • TORONTO • LONDON • SYDNEY • AUCKLAND

RL 4, 008–012

THE UNICORNS GO HAWAIIAN
*A Bantam Book / December 1991*

*Sweet Valley High® and Sweet Valley Twins and Friends are
trademarks of Francine Pascal*

*Conceived by Francine Pascal*

*Produced by Daniel Weiss Associates, Inc.
33 West 17th Street
New York, NY 10011*

*Cover art by James Mathewuse*

*Skylark Books is a registered trademark of Bantam Books,
a division of Bantam Doubleday Dell Publishing Group, Inc.
Registered in U.S. Patent and Trademark Office and elsewhere.*

ISBN 0-553-15948-8

*Published simultaneously in the United States and Canada*

*Bantam Books are published by Bantam Books, a division of Ban-
tam Doubleday Dell Publishing Group, Inc. Its trademark, con-
sisting of the words "Bantam Books" and the portrayal of a
rooster, is Registered in U.S. Patent and Trademark Office and in
other countries. Marca Registrada. Bantam Books, 666 Fifth Ave-
nue, New York, New York 10103*

PRINTED IN THE UNITED STATES OF AMERICA

OPM     0  9  8  7  6  5  4  3  2  1

# The
# Unicorns
# Go
# Hawaiian

# *One*

◇

"Jessica! This looks like potato *soup*, not potato salad!" Mrs. Gerhart cried during cooking class at Sweet Valley Middle School.

"I *like* it that way," Jessica Wakefield replied defensively. "It's an old family recipe."

Mrs. Gerhart frowned, then made a note in her grade book. "The idea was to follow the recipe *I* gave you."

Jessica held up a spoonful of the salad. "Aren't you even going to taste it?"

Mrs. Gerhart shook her head. "I don't think that will be necessary. Maybe you'll have better luck with next week's Jell-O mold."

"I doubt it," Jessica's friend, Mandy Miller, whispered.

The teacher turned her attention to Elizabeth Wakefield's mixing bowl. "Now *that's* what potato salad should look like!" she exclaimed as she dipped her spoon into the salad and sampled it.

"Umm! Perfect! That's an A effort, Elizabeth."
Mrs. Gerhart smiled, then glanced over at Jessica's
mixing bowl. "You know, sometimes it's hard to
believe you two are twins," she said as she patted
Jessica on the shoulder.

Once Mrs. Gerhart was safely out of earshot,
Jessica giggled. It always surprised her when people actually expected her and Elizabeth to *act* alike,
just because they *looked* alike. Right down to the
tiny dimples in their left cheeks, the twins were
perfect copies of each other. Both girls had long
silky hair streaked with gold by the California sunshine, and sparkling blue-green eyes framed by
long, dark lashes.

But when it came to their personalities, Jessica
knew that nobody had difficulty telling the girls
apart. Elizabeth was the more studious and hard-
working twin. She was the editor of the sixth-
grade newspaper, *The Sweet Valley Sixers*, and she
dreamed of becoming a journalist someday. Elizabeth loved to spend her spare time curled up with
a good mystery novel or enjoying the company of
her close friends and family.

Jessica loved spending time with friends, too.
She belonged to the Unicorn Club, an exclusive
group of girls who considered themselves to be
the prettiest and most popular at Sweet Valley
Middle School. In fact, the Unicorns wore purple
every day, the color of royalty, to remind everyone of their special status. Jessica knew that Elizabeth had nicknamed the Unicorns "The Snob

Squad." But despite their differences, Jessica and Elizabeth would always be best friends.

"What did you get on your potato salad, Jessica?" Lila Fowler asked as she joined the group. Lila was one of Jessica's closest friends, and she was also a member of the Unicorns.

"I wasn't crazy enough to ask," Jessica admitted.

Lila looked at the contents of Jessica's bowl and laughed. "You *definitely* win the prize for the ugliest potato salad!"

After school, Jessica invited Mandy Miller over to study for their history test the next day.

Jessica laid her head down on her kitchen table and sighed dramatically. "Mandy, do you realize it's only October? We've got *months* of history tests ahead of us!"

"Maybe we should take another break," Mandy suggested.

Jessica looked at the clock on the microwave. "We've only been studying for four minutes."

"We need to work into it gradually," Mandy replied. "It's like warming up for exercise." She picked up a magazine that was left on the table and began to flip through it. "Hey, look at this! A contest!"

Jessica peered over Mandy's shoulder. " 'The Pineapple People will present the creator of the most unusual pineapple recipe an amazing grand prize,' " she read out loud.

"Let's do it!" Mandy said excitedly. "Let's make the most outrageous pineapple recipe we can think of and send it to the Pineapple People. It says they want something unusual!"

"I've had enough of cooking for one day," Jessica protested. "Plus I'm certainly not a good cook."

"But this is just the opposite of real cooking! We'll throw in whatever we want. It'll be fun, Jess!"

Jessica glanced from her history book to Mandy's expectant face. She had to admit that Mandy's idea sounded like more fun than reading about the Battle of Bunker Hill.

"All right," she agreed at last, shoving aside her textbook. "What'll we make?" Jessica went to the cupboards and swung one open. "Let's see. Anchovies. That's a good start."

"Yuck."

"And chocolate chips. And peppermint extract."

"Gross," Mandy said.

Jessica's eyes lit up with a sudden inspiration. "We'll make potato salad!" she cried. "A potato salad that would make Mrs. Gerhart turn green!"

Mandy giggled. "I thought you'd already done that."

"Very funny." Jessica began pulling more ingredients off the shelves. "This will definitely be the most unusual pineapple recipe in the history of cooking!"

For the next fifteen minutes the girls threw

everything they could find into a large mixing bowl, stirring in a slice of raw potato every now and then.

"It still needs something," Mandy commented at last, as she admired their creation. "Those slices of pineapple look kind of lost in there."

Jessica explored another cupboard and found a bottle of green food coloring. With a wicked grin, she stirred in drops of color until the goopy mess was the color of an emerald.

"What *is* that green stuff?" Elizabeth said as she entered the kitchen.

"Hi, Lizzie," Jessica answered matter-of-factly. "How was your *Sixers* meeting?"

"Never mind my *Sixers* meeting!" Elizabeth exclaimed. "Have you two lost your minds?"

"No, just our appetites," Jessica joked. "What do you think of our creation? We call it the Poisonous Potato Salad." She held up a spoonful of the green glop. "Not even *Steven* would eat this," she said proudly. "And he'll eat *anything!*" Steven, the twins' fourteen-year-old brother, had a notoriously large appetite.

"You're *not* going to enter this contest, are you?" Elizabeth asked as she glanced at the open magazine.

"Of course," Mandy answered. "The Pineapple People wanted something unusual!"

"What's wrong, Elizabeth? Don't you think we'll win?" Jessica asked, laughing.

"That's just it!" Elizabeth exclaimed. "I'm sure you *will* win!"

"And what's wrong with winning?" Jessica asked.

Elizabeth laughed. "What's wrong is that the ad doesn't specify what the winning prize is. I'll bet the prize is a zillion cans of pineapple. And I *hate* pineapple! We'll be eating pineapple for breakfast, lunch, and dinner. We'll probably all turn bright yellow!"

"Don't be such a party pooper, Elizabeth," Jessica said. "Let me see that magazine again."

Elizabeth handed the magazine to Jessica.

Jessica studied the contest ad carefully. "I have one chance in 1,194,239 to win," she reported.

"That's one too many!" Elizabeth said.

Mandy held up a spoonful of the green pasty-looking substance dotted with anchovies, pineapple, and raw potatoes. "I really wouldn't worry too much about our winning, Elizabeth!"

"Hey, what's up?" The three girls turned to see Steven enter the kitchen, a basketball under his arm.

The girls exchanged conspiratorial looks, then smiled. "Try this, Steven," Jessica urged sweetly. "You'll like it."

Steven peeked into the bowl and then cast her a suspicious look. "Who made it?"

"I did," Mandy said quickly.

The girls watched in amazement as Steven reached for a spoon and retrieved a huge helping of their concoction. While Steven swallowed, no one said a word.

"Not bad."

"You don't think there's something a little— *odd* about it?" Mandy ventured. She looked over at Jessica, who was trying very hard not to burst into laughter.

"Odd?" Steven repeated. He tasted another spoonful. "Well, yeah, now that you mention it. It could definitely use a little more salt."

# Two

"Can you believe it's almost Christmas?" Elizabeth asked one Saturday afternoon in late December as the twins entered the Sweet Valley Mall. "It seems like only yesterday that the mall was decorated for Thanksgiving!"

Jessica smiled. "I've been waiting *forever* for Christmas vacation to get here. Just a few more days, and we'll finally be *free!*"

"Yeah, and this is going to be our best vacation *ever*," Elizabeth said. "I can't wait to go skiing!"

The day after Christmas the Wakefield family was heading to the mountains to spend the week at a ski lodge. Both sets of the twins' grandparents were planning to meet them there.

"Do you think learning to ski will be hard?" Elizabeth asked as the twins continued toward the food court.

"Maybe," Jessica answered. "Lila's been telling me horror stories about the first time she went skiing. She claims she came home with twenty-seven bruises."

"She's probably exaggerating."

"I *hope* so," Jessica said quietly. For some reason, she was not nearly as excited about going skiing as Elizabeth was. Skiing meant snow, and snow meant cold, and cold meant thermal underwear and runny noses.

Still, Jessica reminded herself, there was always the part *after* skiing. She tried to imagine herself sitting by a roaring fire while cute guys in ski boots and bright sweaters gathered around to keep her cup of hot cocoa refilled. Maybe she could even skip the skiing part altogether!

"Hey, there's Amy!" Elizabeth cried. Amy Sutton was Elizabeth's closest friend after Jessica. She was standing next to a display of giant candy canes, struggling with two large shopping bags filled to the brim with smaller packages.

"Finishing your Christmas shopping, Amy?" Elizabeth asked as the twins joined her.

Amy brushed a stray lock of blond hair out of her eyes impatiently. "I think I set a new record for speedy gift buying. All I have left now is my dad." She sighed heavily. "Boy, do I hate shopping!"

"*Hate* shopping?" Jessica repeated. "That's impossible!"

"Trust me, Jessica, it's possible. Next year I think I'll just give everybody gift certificates."

"I'll never understand how anyone could hate

to shop!" Jessica continued. "This mall is like my second home. The Unicorns come here practically every weekend!"

Amy jerked her head in the direction of the food court. "I just saw a bunch of Unicorns over by the frozen yogurt stand. There's a really cute guy behind the counter."

Jessica quickly left Elizabeth with Amy and headed toward her friends. Just as Amy had said, the Unicorns were standing in a long line at the frozen yogurt stand.

"This is my second cup of strawberry yogurt," Lila confessed as Jessica joined her. "But it's worth it. The yogurt guy is absolutely adorable!" Lila nodded at Janet Howell, who was ahead of her in line. "Janet's on her fourth cone."

"Third," Janet corrected. "And *I* saw him first, Lila. Besides, he's too old for you." Janet, an eighth grader, was Lila's first cousin. Not only was she the president of the Unicorn Club, she was also considered the prettiest and most popular girl in school, and she never let anyone forget it.

Mary Wallace, a seventh-grade Unicorn, laughed. "I hate to break it to you, guys, but he's not going to ask any of us out just because we like the way he scoops yogurt!"

"It's worth a try," argued Ellen Riteman, a sixth-grade member of the Unicorns.

Jessica stood on her tiptoes to get a look at the yogurt guy, but her view was obstructed by a very tall boy ahead of them wearing a high school letter jacket. "This line sure is slow," she complained. "So where do you guys want to go shopping first?"

Lila shrugged. "I don't really care. I *was* going to get a new outfit for Christmas dinner, but . . ."

"But what?" Jessica pressed.

"But now that I know *Bambi's* going to be there, I don't really care what I wear! Maybe I'll just wear my sweatpants and a smelly old T-shirt."

"Who's Bambi?" Jessica asked.

"You know, the baby deer," Ellen answered. "Thumper's friend."

"Wrong, Ellen," Lila said through gritted teeth. "Bambi is my father's new girlfriend."

Ellen looked puzzled. "Her parents named her after a deer?"

"What's she like?" Jessica asked, ignoring Ellen. Even though Jessica knew that Lila's parents had gotten divorced when Lila was only four, it was still strange to think of Lila's father with a "girlfriend."

"I don't really know what Bambi's like," Lila said sullenly. "I've only talked to her on the phone. She sounds like a real airhead. She actually asked me if I wanted a doll for Christmas!"

"She's coming to your house on Christmas Day?" Mary asked. "Sounds serious."

"That's what I'm afraid of," Lila admitted. "Daddy says he really wants Bambi and I to get to know each other. We have to spend the *whole day* together." Lila crossed her arms over her chest. "It just isn't fair. I hardly ever get to see my father, and then when I do, I have to share him with a perfect stranger."

Jessica nodded sympathetically. Mr. Fowler, who was one of the wealthiest men in Sweet Valley, traveled frequently on business. He constantly spoiled Lila to make up for all the time they spent apart. Although Jessica was sometimes jealous of Lila's wealth, she was glad she had a father, not to mention a mother, who was always there for her.

"I know what I'm going to do," Lila said brightly. "I'm going to buy myself the most expensive outfit I can find to wear on Christmas Day. Daddy gave me his credit card today, so the sky's the limit!" She paused. "Well, almost."

"That's the spirit," Jessica said encouragingly.

"Bambi," Ellen repeated, shaking her head. "Are you sure that's her *real* name?" Ellen giggled, and Mary delivered a swift kick to her shin. Suddenly, Lila stepped out of line.

"What about your yogurt?" Jessica asked.

Lila shrugged. "I lost my appetite."

"What about the yogurt *guy*?" Janet said.

"He's all yours," Lila answered. "Meet me at Kendall's when you're finished."

"What department in Kendall's?" Mary asked.

"Dresses," Lila replied with a faint smile. "Outrageously Expensive Dresses."

Without another word, she disappeared into the crowd.

Jessica was walking into homeroom on the last day before Christmas vacation when Lila came dashing down the hall, waving something in the air. She grabbed Jessica by the arm and yanked her into the hallway.

"Read this," Lila commanded breathlessly. She shoved a copy of *It Takes a Woman* magazine into Jessica's hand.

"But why?" Jessica demanded.

"Just read the page it's open to." Lila leaned against a locker, struggling to catch her breath.

" 'Look Years Younger in Minutes,' " Jessica read aloud.

"The *other* page."

" 'Tips for Lowering Your Cholesterol,' " Jessica read obediently. She cast a sidelong glance at Lila. "Do you *really* read this magazine?"

Lila threw up her hands in frustration. "Don't you get it? Look at the pineapple ad, dummy. You won!"

"Won?"

"I was thumbing through this today during breakfast. If our housekeeper hadn't left it open on the table, I might never have seen it. But fortunately for you, I did! I tried to call you at home, but you'd already left for school." Lila paused. "Can you believe it?"

Overhead, the bell jangled loudly. Jessica narrowed her eyes. Maybe the stress of the holiday season was getting to Lila. She wasn't making *any* sense.

Jessica took a step toward the entrance to Mr. Davis's room.

"Where do you think *you're* going?" Lila demanded. "Don't you get it? You won the Pineapple People contest! That disgusting recipe you and Mandy entered two months ago actually won the grand prize!" Lila lowered her voice to a whisper. "And do you have any idea what the grand prize *is*?"

"A zillion cans of pineapple?"

"A trip to Hawaii for the winner and two friends!" Lila hissed.

"Hawaii?" Jessica echoed. "Islands and volcanoes and hula dancers—*that* Hawaii?" Was it possible she *had* really won that silly contest?

"You've got to get to a phone, Jess," Lila shouted as she began to drag Jessica down the hallway. "You have to claim the prize by calling the magazine before eleven A.M. on December twenty-first."

"That's today!" Jessica cried. She glanced up at the clock in the hallway. "But it's only seven fifty-five—"

"Eleven, Eastern Standard Time," Lila interrupted. "That's eight, here in California. It's a different time zone."

"Are you sure?"

"Positive." Lila nodded her head forcefully.

"I call my father whenever he's in New York on business. You've only got five minutes, Jessica!"

The girls raced toward the pay phone in the lobby, their footsteps echoing loudly in the empty hallways. "Guess what the consolation prize is if you *don't* call in time?" Lila said breathlessly as they ran. "Pineapple! Two hundred cans of pineapple!"

When they got to the pay phone, Jessica stopped dead in her tracks. A little hand-lettered sign taped to the pay phone read OUT OF ORDER.

"It's *always* out of order!" Lila complained. "Why can't they fix it once, and—"

"The principal's office!" Jessica interrupted.

The clock on the wall read 7:58 by the time the girls burst through the doors into Mr. Clark's office.

"The phone!" Jessica gasped, nearly colliding with the secretary's desk. "I've got to use the phone!"

Mrs. Knight looked up in surprise. "Is this some kind of emergency, Jessica?"

"I'd call two hundred cans of pineapple an emergency, wouldn't you?" Lila demanded.

"If I don't make a long-distance call to New York in the next minute, I won't get to go to Hawaii," Jessica blurted out.

"The school can't afford to pay for your personal long-distance telephone calls," Mrs. Knight said sternly, peering at Jessica over her wire-rimmed glasses. "I'd have to get your parents' permission first. In any case, you're about to be late for class, ladies."

"Look at this!" Lila cried in exasperation, shoving her copy of *It Takes a Woman* under Mrs. Knight's nose.

" 'Look Years Younger in Minutes,' " Mrs. Knight read aloud. She furrowed her brow. "What exactly is your point, Lila?"

"No, no! The pineapple ad! See Jessica's name?"

Jessica glanced at Mrs. Knight's clock and her heart seemed to stop. "It's seven fifty-nine!"

"My, my," Mrs. Knight exclaimed. "I had no idea you were such a gourmet, Jessica!" She waved over to Mr. Edwards, the vice principal, who was passing by carrying a cup of coffee. "Would you look at this, Jim!" she said, pointing to Jessica's name in the magazine. "Our very own Jessica Wakefield is going to Hawaii!"

"Not unless she uses your phone!" Lila cried, grabbing the receiver and passing it to Jessica. "What's the number, Mrs. Knight? There, at the bottom of the ad."

Mrs. Knight scanned the ad, then consulted her watch. "Oh my," she said. "Now I see what you mean!" Quickly she read off the phone number, and Lila punched the numbers into the phone.

For a moment, the office was silent, all eyes on Jessica. "Hello?" she said at last. "My name is

Jessica Wakefield, and I won your pineapple recipe contest."

"Please hold, will you?" said a voice at the other end of the line.

Suddenly the eight o'clock bell rang, so loudly that everyone in the office jumped. Jessica looked up at the clock and groaned.

"What if I'm too late?" Jessica whispered.

Lila didn't answer. She was holding her breath. Mrs. Knight and Mr. Edwards crossed their fingers.

Suddenly, a woman's voice came on the line. "Congratulations, Ms. Wakefield," said the woman. "Or should I say 'Aloha'?"

Jessica dropped the receiver onto Mrs. Knight's desk. "I won!" she screamed. "I'm going to Hawaii!"

# *Three*

◇

"Hawaii! Can you believe it?" Jessica marveled as she and Lila walked back to homeroom.

"Just think," Lila said importantly. "If I hadn't been bored enough at breakfast to look at that magazine, you might never have known you won!"

"I would have when the two hundred cans of pineapple arrived on my doorstep!" Jessica replied.

"When do you get the tickets?"

"They're sending me the tickets and the hotel information by special mail," Jessica replied. "It should arrive tomorrow."

Just as the girls approached Mr. Davis's room, the bell rang. "I'm glad Mr. Edwards wrote us an excuse," Lila said. "Otherwise, Mr. Davis would never believe why we missed homeroom!"

As students began to stream out of class, Lila ran up to Mr. Davis and presented him with their written excuses. Jessica waited in the hallway for Elizabeth to pass by.

Jessica smiled slyly when she spotted her twin. "Lizzie," she began, "how do you feel about Hawaii?"

"Hawaii?"

"Yeah. You know—hula skirts, volcanoes, luaus, *pineapples*."

"Pineapples?"

"The kind I put in my Poisonous Potato Salad."

Elizabeth's face wore a puzzled expression for a moment. And then her mouth dropped open, and she let her backpack fall to the floor with a thud. "You won, didn't you?" she whispered. "I *knew* you'd win that pineapple contest! I *told* you so!"

"Fortunately, I claimed my grand prize in the nick of time," Jessica said. "Tickets for me and two friends to Hawaii! For a whole week! What a great Christmas vacation!"

Elizabeth hugged Jessica. "This is incredible! You and I are going to Hawaii, Jess!"

"You must have heard the news," Lila said as she joined them. "Jess wouldn't have known if it weren't for me!"

"But that *disgusting* pineapple recipe?" Elizabeth said. "I just don't see how they'd award *you* the grand prize, Jess."

"Me, either. But don't forget that Steven liked it. Maybe it wasn't so bad after all."

Suddenly, Elizabeth's smile evaporated. "Oh, no! How could we have forgotten?" she said softly. "What about our ski vacation?"

"We can go skiing some other time," Jessica replied airily. "How often do you get a chance to go to Hawaii?"

"It's not skiing I was thinking about," Elizabeth said glumly. "It's grandparents."

Their grandparents! Jessica had completely forgotten! "I guess they'd be kind of disappointed if we weren't there, huh?" Jessica asked, her shoulders sagging.

Elizabeth nodded. "I'd feel awful disappointing them."

"So they don't get to see you," Lila interjected impatiently. "So what? *I* see you two every day, and trust me, it's no big deal."

"But they've been looking forward to this ski trip for months," Elizabeth explained.

"Send a postcard from Hawaii," Lila advised. "That's what I do with *my* grandparents. Postcards once or twice a year, and they're happy."

"I don't think a postcard will do it," Jessica said quietly. It just wasn't fair. She had only known about her fabulous trip for a few minutes, and already it was beginning to look as if it would never happen.

"Jessica!" somebody shrieked.

Jessica spun around to see Mandy sprinting toward her.

"I just heard the most incredible rumor!" Mandy cried. "Caroline Pearce was in the principal's office this morning, and she says Mrs. Knight told her this amazing story about you going to Hawaii. But I know it can't be true, because that green glop we made could *never* have won—"

"It's true," Jessica confirmed.

Mandy grabbed Jessica's arm and began to pull her down the hallway.

"Wait!" Jessica protested. "Lizzie and I need to figure out—"

"Whatever it is, it can wait!" Mandy exclaimed. "Right now, you and I are going to see Mrs. Gerhart."

"Why?"

"Because I want to see her face when you tell her that your potato salad just won the grand prize in a cooking contest! I've never seen a teacher faint before!"

"So what are we going to do about the ski trip?" Jessica asked Elizabeth as they sat down together at lunch. It was the first time they had had a chance to talk since that morning. Usually Jessica sat at the Unicorner, the Unicorns' special table, but today she needed time to sort things out with Elizabeth.

"Well, I've been giving it a lot of thought," Elizabeth said as she unwrapped a sandwich, "and I think that *I* should go skiing and that *you* should go to Hawaii. That way our grandparents will at least be able to see one of us."

"But Lizzie!" Jessica exclaimed. "Vacation wouldn't be the same without you! And it's not fair for you to get stuck in a stuffy old ski lodge while I get to sun myself on a beautiful Hawaiian beach!"

Elizabeth grinned. "It's not as if I'll be suffering, Jess. And the truth is, I wanted to go skiing more than you did."

"But think of all the cute Hawaiian guys you could meet!" Jessica protested.

"I'm sure there are going to be plenty of cute guys in the mountains, too," Elizabeth pointed out. "Besides, I *did* tell you I didn't want anything to do with the pineapple prize."

"But that's when you thought I was going to win zillions of cans of pineapple." Jessica rested her chin in her hand and sighed. She and Elizabeth had always spent their vacations together. It didn't seem right for them to split up now. Still, she really couldn't see any alternative. They couldn't disappoint their grandparents. And the woman from the magazine had said that the contest rules required Jessica to take the Hawaii trip within sixty days. Christmas vacation would be her only chance to go.

"I suppose you're right, Elizabeth," Jessica admitted at last. "But who am I going to ask to go with me?"

"Well, Mandy, of course," Elizabeth said. "After all, she helped you create your masterpiece."

"I've already asked Mandy," Jessica said. Then she glanced over at the Unicorner. "I wish there was some way I could invite all the Unicorns. It's going to be hard to pick just one."

"There's Lila," Elizabeth suggested. "She *did* find your name in the magazine."

"I think Lila already assumes she's going," Jessica whispered. "But I haven't officially invited her yet. She already gets to travel all over the world, so I thought it might be nice to invite someone else. Someone the trip would mean more to."

"How about Mary Wallace? I don't think she's ever traveled outside the state," Elizabeth said. "She'd be thrilled if you asked her."

"Lizzie, that's perfect!" Jessica jumped up, called Mary's name, and motioned her over to join her.

"What's up, Jess?" Mary asked when she had arrived. "Hey, I heard about your trip. You must be so excited!"

"I can't wait!" Jessica replied. "And I was just wondering about your plans for Christmas vacation."

Mary shrugged. "Well, I've got some pretty exciting stuff lined up. My mom has been bugging me for months to clean out my closet. And I thought I might go for broke and clean under my bed while I'm at it." She tossed her long blond hair over her shoulder. "I lead a pretty glamorous life!"

Jessica grinned. She felt a little like Santa Claus. "Too bad," she said. "I was hoping you might want to go to Hawaii with me. But I can understand how you wouldn't want to pass up that closet cleaning, Mary. Maybe some other time."

"Hawaii!" Mary cried. "You want *me* to go to Hawaii with you?"

"With me and Mandy, actually."

"Jessica!" Mary exclaimed, "this is the best Christmas present I've *ever* gotten! Wait'll everybody hears!"

Before Jessica could say another word, Mary dashed back to the Unicorner to share her news. "I hope the rest of the group isn't too jealous," Jessica whispered to Elizabeth.

Just then, the twins saw Lila shove back her chair with a loud metallic scrape. She tossed down a bag of Cheez Doodles and stomped down the aisle, her face frozen in a frown. When she passed Jessica she paused just long enough to mutter, "Some friend *you* are, Jessica Wakefield!"

Jessica watched Lila charge out of the cafeteria, then turned back to Elizabeth. "I think she took it pretty well," she remarked with a smile.

Still, Jessica did feel a bit guilty. After all, Lila *was* her best friend, after Elizabeth. And she *had* been having a rough time of it lately, with Bambi hanging around her father.

But the fact was that Lila had already been to Hawaii, and Mary and Mandy had not. Jessica thought she was just being fair. And if she felt a

teeny bit good about Lila's obvious jealousy—
well, that was only natural, wasn't it? Lila had
made Jessica jealous of her plenty of times in the
past. For once, it was nice to change places.

"Hawaii!" Mr. and Mrs. Wakefield exclaimed
later that night.

"Remember that recipe contest Mandy and I
entered?" Jessica explained. "Well, this morning
I found out that I won! A week in Hawaii, with
all expenses paid, for me and two of my friends.
I already invited Mandy and Mary. Lizzie and I
decided that one of us had to go skiing so that
Grandma and Grandpa Robertson and Grandma
and Grandpa Wakefield wouldn't be too disappointed."

Jessica paused, waiting for her parents to be as
thrilled as all her friends at school had been. But
when she looked at their faces, all she saw was
something that looked an awful lot like annoyance.

"I'm very proud of you, Jess," Mr. Wakefield
said at last. "I had no idea we had a budding chef
in our midst. But I'm afraid Hawaii is out of the
question. We couldn't let you go without a chaperon, honey."

Jessica stared at her father in disbelief. *What
was he saying?*

# *Four*

◇

Jessica lay back on her bed and wiped away a stray tear. "My life is ruined! Totally and completely ruined!"

"I know how disappointed you are, Jess," Elizabeth said comfortingly. "But it's not the end of the world."

Jessica propped herself up on her elbows. "But going to Hawaii has always been my dream, Lizzie!"

"I've never heard you mention Hawaii before," Elizabeth pointed out.

"My *secret* dream," Jessica explained. "For as long as I can remember, I've wanted to visit a foreign country."

"Hawaii's a state, Jess. It's part of the United States."

Jessica rolled her eyes. "I *know* that. I meant that it *seems* like a foreign country, because it's so exotic. It has palm trees—"

"So do we."

"And surfers."

"So do we."

"And *volcanoes*! You can't tell me we have any volcanoes here in Sweet Valley!"

Elizabeth grinned and sat down next to Jessica on her bed. "How about the time when the faucet blew? That was pretty close to a volcanic eruption! I'm sorry, Jess. Look, maybe Mom and Dad will change their minds."

Jessica stared up at the ceiling and sighed. "Mom and Dad won't change their minds. They never do. It's some kind of parent law."

"Jessica! Telephone!" Steven yelled from downstairs.

"What if it's Mandy or Mary?" Jessica asked, panicked. "What will I tell them?"

"The truth, I suppose."

"But they'll think I'm such a baby!" Jessica whined. "I'll never live this down!" Reluctantly, she dragged herself off the bed and headed for the telephone in the hallway.

"Hello?" she said quietly.

"Jess? It's Lila. And have I got some incredible news!"

"Me, too," Jessica replied sullenly.

"You go first," Lila said brightly.

"No, you." *There's no point in rushing the bad news*, Jessica thought.

"This is just so exciting!" Lila gushed. "When I told my dad about your trip to Hawaii, and about how you asked Mandy and Mary when *I* should have been your first choice—"

"Lila—" Jessica began, but Lila would not let her finish.

"Well, naturally, he felt incredibly sorry for me," she continued. "*Especially* when I turned on the tears!"

*Too bad that doesn't work on all parents*, Jessica thought bitterly.

"So Daddy said he would send me to Hawaii, too!" Lila exclaimed.

Jessica slumped to the floor in a pathetic heap while Lila prattled on.

"And the best part is," Lila continued in her annoyingly perky voice, "Daddy's even going to pay for Ellen and Janet to go along, too!"

"All three of you?" Jessica repeated dully.

"Well, Daddy's going, too," Lila said. "He's got business to do in Maui right after Christmas, so he volunteered to be our chaperon. Don't worry, though. You know how I've got him wrapped around my little finger. He'll be easy to get rid of when we want to have some fun."

*Chaperon.* Suddenly Jessica realized the true meaning of that wonderful word. If Mr. Fowler was going to chaperon, Jessica's parents would *have* to let her go to Hawaii. It was a miracle!

"Lila, you're incredible!" Jessica exclaimed.

"Why, yes, I know—"

"I have to hang up now," Jessica interrupted. "Is your dad at home now?"

"He's in the sauna," Lila replied. "Why?"

"How long does that take?"

"*I* don't know, Jessica. It's hard to say. If you stay in too long, you turn into a prune."

"Is there a phone in the sauna room?"

"There's a phone in every room of our house," Lila answered proudly.

"Good. Because I have a feeling my dad will be calling your dad *very* soon!"

Half an hour later, Mr. Wakefield hung up the phone after a long conversation with Lila's father. Jessica sat in the kitchen with the rest of the family, waiting to hear her parents' decision. Underneath the kitchen table, she had her fingers crossed for good luck.

"I'm still not entirely convinced about this trip," Mr. Wakefield said at last. "George Fowler hardly spends any time with his daughter here in Sweet Valley. How can we be sure he'll keep an eye on Lila and a group of her friends in Hawaii?"

Mrs. Wakefield nodded. "That's a good point. I've never thought Lila was very well supervised."

"But that's exactly why you can be sure he'll be a great chaperon!" Jessica argued. "Mr. Fowler feels so guilty about all the time he spends away from Lila that he probably figures the trip to Hawaii's the perfect chance to make it up to her.

He'll probably be with us every minute of the day!"

"Jessica's right," Elizabeth agreed. "And if you're worried, Jessica could call you every day to let you know she's OK."

"Twice a day," Jessica added. "Three times a day, even."

Mr. and Mrs. Wakefield looked at each other and smiled. "Well, I suppose, under the circumstances, we could let you go," Mr. Wakefield said. "If you promise to call often."

"Thank you!" Jessica cried, jumping from her chair to hug first her father, then her mother. "Thank you so much!"

"We expect you to behave responsibly," Mrs. Wakefield warned.

"That'll be a first," Steven joked.

"I will, I will!" Jessica vowed.

Hawaii! She was actually going to Hawaii! *Thank you Mr. Fowler*, she thought. Her trip had been saved!

"You two are the very best parents in the whole world!"

"How many suitcases are you bringing, anyway?" Mandy asked the following afternoon.

Lila and Mandy were sitting on Jessica's bedroom floor, watching while Jessica tried to decide what to bring to Hawaii.

"I'm bringing two big suitcases, a garment

bag, my cosmetics bag, and, of course, my carry-on luggage," Lila said as she carefully filed a nail.

"I'm just going to throw a bunch of stuff in a duffel bag," Mandy said.

"What about wrinkles?" Lila asked.

"Wrinkles add character," Mandy replied.

Jessica stared forlornly into her closet. Her friends were no help at all.

"Come on, Jess. Just throw some stuff in your suitcase and stop worrying about it," Mandy urged. "Hawaii's a very casual place."

"How would you know, Mandy?" Lila asked haughtily. "I'm the only one in the group who's actually *been* to Hawaii. Don't you remember? My father and I spent a long weekend there a few months ago. Actually, Jessica, you should bring something dressy," Lila instructed. "I'm sure Daddy will be taking us out to some very fancy restaurants." She tossed her nail file aside angrily. "Without *her*, I hope."

"Her?" Jessica repeated.

"Who's her?" Mandy asked.

"*Bambi*," Lila grumbled. "I just found out this morning that my dad decided to ask Bambi along on *our* trip. Can you believe it? Like it isn't bad enough that I have to share Christmas Day with her! Now I have to share my vacation, too."

"Maybe it won't be so bad," Mandy said hopefully. "You might even like her, Lila."

"No way!" Lila shook her head forcefully. "I

*refuse* to like her. She's ruining my Christmas vacation. Besides, she's a bimbo."

Jessica tossed a pair of shorts into her suitcase. "How do you know she's a bimbo?"

"Well—" Lila seemed to hesitate. "Well, she's an actress, for starters!"

"What do you mean by *that*?" Mandy, who was a member of the Drama Club, demanded.

"I don't mean *all* actresses are airheads," Lila said quickly. "But I can tell from the way she sounds on the phone. You'll see."

"But she's an *actress*, Lila," Jessica argued. "Think of the people she could introduce us to! Maybe we could visit the set of one of her movies!"

"She hasn't made any movies, Jessica," Lila snapped. "She hasn't even made any commercials. Bambi just auditions for roles. She never *gets* any of them."

"Oh," Jessica said, a little deflated.

"There's one good thing, though," Lila said. "Daddy says Bambi can't stay with us for the entire week. She's got to come back to California to audition for some stupid part which," Lila added with a spiteful smile, "she undoubtedly *won't* get!"

Jessica shrugged and turned her attention to her closet again. She thought Lila was being a little hard on Bambi. As far as Jessica was concerned, an aspiring actress was better than no actress at all. "How about this?" Jessica asked, holding up one of her favorite purple skirts.

Lila and Mandy both shook their heads.

Jessica sighed with frustration. Maybe she would just bring her bathing suit and nothing else. What more could she really need?

# Five

◇

"Did you pack suntan lotion?" Mrs. Wakefield asked Jessica on the Wednesday morning she was to leave for Hawaii.

Jessica nodded.

Mrs. Wakefield turned to Elizabeth, who was dragging her own heavy suitcase across the living-room rug. "Elizabeth, did you remember to pack your mittens?"

Jessica laughed. "You and I had better not mix up our suitcases, Lizzie. I definitely won't be needing mittens where *I'm* going!"

She walked past the Christmas tree and smiled. Yesterday had been wonderful. Remembering the gifts and cookies and carols, Jessica found it hard to believe that Christmas had only been yesterday—and harder still to believe that in only a few minutes, she would be on her way to Hawaii!

Jessica helped Elizabeth put her suitcase into

the family's van. "I still feel sort of guilty," Jessica confessed. "While I'm living it up in Hawaii, you'll be—"

"Living it up in the mountains," Elizabeth finished. "I'm as excited about going skiing as you are about going to Hawaii, Jess."

Jessica leaned against the van. "Still, it's going to seem strange not having you with me."

"I'll go with you the next time you win a contest," Elizabeth vowed. "When's Mr. Fowler coming to pick you up?"

"Any minute now. I'm the last stop before we head for the airport."

"Are you all packed?"

Jessica giggled. "I've been packed for days!" she exclaimed. "Hey, check out those limousines!" She pointed up the street toward two long, shiny black cars.

To Jessica's surprise, the limousines stopped right in front of her house.

One of the car's dark tinted windows eased down, and suddenly Jessica heard a familiar voice. "Get the lead out, Jessica!" Lila cried. "We're going to miss our plane!" The window closed before Jessica could form a response.

While the driver loaded Jessica's suitcase into the first limousine, Mr. Fowler, a tall man wearing a navy blue blazer, got out of the second limousine and greeted Mr. and Mrs. Wakefield. After they spoke for a few minutes, Mr. Fowler returned to his limousine.

"Well, I guess this is it," Jessica said as she gave everyone a quick hug.

"Call us as soon as you get there, honey," Mrs. Wakefield reminded Jessica.

"And send me a postcard," Elizabeth added.

"Send me a surfboard," Steven joked.

"Jessica!" Lila screeched. "Hurry up, already!"

After one last round of hugs, Jessica ran to the limousine, where the driver held open the door for her. "Thanks, uh—what's your name, anyway?" Jessica said.

"Gerald, Miss."

"Well, thanks, Gerald," Jessica said as she slid into the cool dark interior of the car. Mary, Mandy, Ellen, Janet, and Lila were sitting on the wide leather seats.

"Aloha!" Mandy said. "That means hello *or* goodbye. Lila taught us."

"Step on it, Gerald," Lila demanded.

Gerald gave a slight nod. "Yes, Miss."

Jessica waved to her family, but she wasn't sure they could see her through the tinted-glass window.

"Can you believe we're going to the airport in a limousine?" Janet exclaimed. "I feel like a princess or something."

Lila made a show of yawning. "Daddy just thought it would be faster this day. It's really no big deal."

"No big deal?" Mandy cried. "You call a car

with a TV, a stereo, a telephone, and a refrigerator *no big deal*? It sure beats my mom's rusty old Dodge!"

"I can't believe how big this car is," Jessica marveled.

"Actually, it's a little cramped," Lila said. "That's why Daddy and Bambi took a separate limo."

"How was Christmas?" Jessica asked Lila.

"I'll tell you how Christmas was," Lila said defiantly. "It was *awful*. Do you know what she gave me?" Lila held out her hand, a sneer on her lips. On her wrist was a small gold charm bracelet with little hearts dangling from it.

"Cute," Jessica said.

"Not cute," Lila corrected. *"Cheap."*

"I saw those at Kendall's," Ellen said. "They were about five dollars."

"Exactly my point," Lila said.

"But it's the thought that counts, Lila," Mandy said. "Maybe Bambi couldn't afford any more than that."

Lila looked out the window, obviously unconvinced.

Jessica almost hated to see the car trip end, but the airport proved to be even more exciting. The terminal was bustling with people. Computerized signs listed the times when planes would be arriving and taking off. Jessica had never realized that at any one time so many people were coming and going in the sky!

While Gerald took care of their luggage, Mr. Fowler gathered the girls together when they had piled out of the car. Bambi was leaning on his arm. She had short blond hair, big green eyes, and, Jessica noted, extremely well-applied makeup. She would have to ask Bambi to give her a few eye-shadow tips during their stay in Hawaii.

"For those of you who don't already know me," Mr. Fowler said, "I'm George Fowler—Lila's dad—and this is Bambi Mifflin."

Jessica glanced over at Lila, who was glaring at her father.

"I—well, *we*, really—are going to be your chaperons for the next seven days," Mr. Fowler continued. He looked at the group with an expression of uncertainty. "I suppose everybody should introduce herself," he said at last. "Lila, why don't you do the honors?"

"I think you've already met everyone, Daddy."

"I could use a little refresher course. Besides," he added, "Bambi would like to meet your friends."

Lila sighed loudly. "Oh, all right." She pointed around the circle of girls. "Jessica, Mary, Mandy, Ellen, Janet. Satisfied?"

"Hi, girls," Bambi said brightly.

"Are you really an actress?" Jessica asked.

"Well, I'm trying," Bambi replied.

"Daddy, can we please go now?" Lila whined. "We're going to miss our plane!"

"Of course," Mr. Fowler said. He glanced at

his gold watch and nodded. "We're right on schedule. Follow me, ladies."

Once they were checked in, the girls sat in a small waiting area. Through the floor-to-ceiling windows they could see their jet being prepared for takeoff.

"How many of you have flown before?" Bambi asked. "Other than Lila, of course. From what I understand, she's quite the world traveler."

Lila studied her nails.

"I flew to New Orleans to visit my grandparents the summer before last," Janet said importantly.

"I flew to Tucson when I was only six months old!" Mandy chimed in.

When it was finally time to board the plane, the girls lined up behind Mr. Fowler and Bambi and walked down a long corridor directly to the door of the plane.

"Hello," said a stewardess as Jessica stepped on board.

"Welcome," she said to Mandy.

"They're so friendly!" Mandy whispered.

"Oh, Mandy, they say hello to everybody!" Lila replied. "They have to. It's their job."

"I love their outfits!" Ellen remarked as she followed Lila into the body of the plane.

"Please, Ellen!" Lila scoffed.

"That's OK, Ellen," Bambi said. "I like them, too."

A steward helped the group find their seats.

Jessica, as the official contest winner, insisted on a window seat. Mandy sat beside her.

Ellen wanted to be as far from the window as possible. She looked a little pale when the stewardess explained safety procedures to the passengers. And when the stewardess demonstrated how to use an oxygen mask, Ellen covered her eyes. Jessica stifled a giggle.

A few seconds later, a man's voice came over the loudspeaker. "Good morning, folks," he said cheerfully. "This is your captain speaking. We'll be taking off in just a few minutes. Temperature in sunny Honolulu right now is a beautiful seventy-eight degrees, and we're expecting clear skies with a few scattered clouds all the way to Hawaii. Relax and enjoy your trip."

Jessica glanced across the aisle at Ellen, who was now clutching her armrests so tightly that her knuckles were white. "I think Ellen's a little nervous," she whispered to Mandy.

"Who isn't?" Mandy said, and Jessica nodded. There were a few butterflies fluttering around in her own stomach.

Jessica turned toward the window. The terminal building seemed to be rolling away, and suddenly Jessica realized that *she* was the one who was moving. While the girls watched, planes of all sizes took off and landed around them.

Then it was their turn. The jet let out a massive roar and began lumbering down the runway. "Here comes the best part!" Lila said excitedly.

Ellen closed her eyes and gritted her teeth, but Jessica continued to look out the window, hypnotized by the images whizzing past in a blur. Faster and faster they went, until suddenly Jessica felt the jet lift into the air.

Below her, houses and cars and swimming pools shrank to dollhouse size. Was Sweet Valley down there somewhere?

Mandy gave her a nudge. "Amazing, huh?" she whispered.

Jessica nodded and peered across the aisle. Ellen had finally opened her eyes, and she, too, was staring out the window as the world grew smaller and smaller.

Later, there would be a movie, stereo headphones for music, little packs of macadamia nuts, and fancy lunches in plastic trays. But Jessica knew she would always remember most the moment when she looked out the window to say goodbye to Sweet Valley, and all she could see below her was a carpet made of clouds.

# Six

◇

"We're in Hawaii!" Jessica cried. She stepped out of the plane into the brilliant sunshine and made her way down a long flight of portable metal stairs.

Lila joined Jessica at the foot of the stairs and donned a pair of designer sunglasses. "We're in Maui, actually," she corrected.

"Maui?" Ellen asked. "Did we land in the wrong place?"

Mary shielded her eyes from the sun. "Hawaii's made up of eight big islands and lots of little ones," she explained.

"Mary! I had no idea you were so smart!" Ellen exclaimed.

Mary rolled her eyes. "How flattering!" She pulled a small paperback book out of her carry-on bag. "Actually, I was reading my guidebook on the plane while you were busy being terrified, Ellen."

"I was *not* terrified!" Ellen protested. "I was *concerned*."

"Daddy says flying's safer than riding a bike," Lila said, watching as Mr. Fowler and Bambi climbed down the stairs.

"Let's go, girls!" Mr. Fowler said.

"But what about our bags?" Ellen asked.

"The baggage carriers will bring them inside the terminal," Mr. Fowler replied.

As they entered the terminal building, a pretty woman carrying beautiful necklaces made of exotic, colorful flowers approached the group.

"Aloha," she said as she placed one of the necklaces around Bambi's neck.

"Aloha to you, too!" Bambi exclaimed.

"These are called *leis*," the woman explained. "It's the custom here to welcome visitors with a garland of flowers." She presented everyone with a different colored lei.

Jessica sighed with pleasure as the woman placed the lei around her neck. *I have a feeling this is going to be a vacation I'll never forget!* she thought.

An hour later, after a brief ride in a shuttle bus, the group arrived at their hotel. "I'm never leaving," Jessica said as she swept into her room behind a bellhop in a bright green uniform. "Not ever!"

Lila dashed out to the balcony, which overlooked a sparkling white sand beach. "What a view!" she exclaimed. "We're eighteen stories up!"

"Hey, look what's in the closet!" Ellen called.

"Robes!" She put on a thick white terry-cloth robe and modeled it for the girls.

"That's not all!" Jessica called from the bathroom. She came out and displayed a wicker basket containing tiny bottles of shampoo, conditioner, and moisturizer. "There's even a little sewing kit!" she marveled. "These hotel people think of everything!"

A door next to one of the beds swung open, and Mary appeared. "Adjoining rooms," she pronounced. "Perfect!"

Mandy and Janet followed Mary into the room. Janet was wearing a white robe, too. "Can we keep these?" she asked.

The bellhop shook his head and grinned.

"No, Janet," Lila said patiently. "You can keep the little shampoos and stuff, though."

"Ladies? Is there anything else I can get you?" the bellhop asked.

"That will be all for now," Lila said with a wave of her hand. "My father will take care of your tip."

Mandy pulled open a desk drawer. "They even give you stationery!" she exclaimed.

Jessica fell down onto one of the king-size beds and sighed. "This is heaven," she said.

"Wait'll you see the beaches," Lila said confidently. "And the adorable guys!"

There was a knock at the door. "Come in!" Mandy yelled.

Bambi stepped inside. "Are you girls getting settled?" she asked.

"This place is incredible!" Mary said excitedly.

"Isn't it?" Bambi agreed. "I think I'm as excited as you guys are," she admitted. "This is my first trip to Hawaii, too." Bambi smiled at Lila, but her smile was not returned. "I'm hoping Lila can give us all some pointers on where to go and what to see."

"There are guidebooks in the lobby," Lila said frostily.

"Yes, well . . ." Bambi began. She looked over at Jessica. "Have you decided on sleeping arrangements?"

"Janet, Mary, and Mandy are going to be in the room next door," Jessica answered. "And Lila, Ellen, and I will be in here." She grinned. "Unless Lila snores too loudly."

"I've never snored in my life, Jessica Wakefield!" Lila protested defiantly.

"How about at that sleepover at Janet's house during Thanksgiving vacation?" Mandy asked. "You kept us up all night, Lila!"

"I *did* not!" Lila cried, her cheeks flaming.

"Sounded just like a hog," Mandy continued.

Bambi laughed with the rest of the group, but she gave Lila a friendly pat on the back. "They're just giving you a hard time, Lila," she said with a smile.

"*I* know that," Lila shot back. "They're *my*

friends, after all. Don't you think I know when my friends are being obnoxious?"

"Ladies? May I join you?" Mr. Fowler called from the hallway.

"Come on in," Bambi answered.

Mr. Fowler had changed into a gray suit and was carrying a leather briefcase. "I'm off to a business meeting, girls," he said. "It should last most of the day. I thought we'd get together for dinner here in the hotel. Let's meet about six-thirty." He winked at Lila. "We'll have ourselves a little quality time then. OK, honey?"

Lila nodded sullenly.

Mr. Fowler cleared his throat. "Now, I suppose, as your official chaperon, I should lay down some ground rules." He tapped his chin with his finger. "Hm," he murmured. "Ground rules."

Jessica could not wait to hear what Mr. Fowler would say next. As far as she knew, Lila never had to follow any sort of rules, other than the one about not going over the limit on her father's credit cards.

Mr. Fowler sat down on the edge of one of the beds while the group watched him expectantly. His brow was furrowed and he seemed to be concentrating very hard. Suddenly his eyes lit up. "To start with, I don't want you spending your money on inferior quality merchandise," he instructed forcefully. "Shop carefully, and avoid tacky souvenir peddlers." He crossed his arms over his chest, apparently satisfied.

For a moment, nobody spoke. "Is—is that it?" Mandy finally ventured.

"Trust me, it's good advice," Mr. Fowler said. He stood abruptly.

"Why don't I keep an eye on the girls?" Bambi suggested. "I still remember how *I* used to get into trouble at their age!"

"That's a fine idea," Mr. Fowler said eagerly. Jessica thought he looked relieved. "Any problems, report to Bambi." He glanced at his watch. "Well, I'm off." He gave Bambi a kiss on the cheek, then stepped over to Lila and kissed her on the top of her head. "Aloha, girls," he said as he strode out of the room.

Bambi shrugged. "Well, I guess I'll be going, too. My room is number 1823, across the hall. Lila's dad's room is at the very end of the hall." She smiled. "I think he wanted to get as far away as possible from us girls!"

Everyone laughed except Lila. "If you need me, I'll be on the beach in front of the hotel working on my tan later this afternoon," Bambi continued. "Plan on meeting back here for dinner at six-thirty. In the meantime, be careful who you talk to, and don't wander too far off, OK?"

The girls nodded, and when Bambi left, they got ready to hit the beach. "You know, Bambi seems pretty nice to me, Lila," Jessica said carefully. "Maybe you two just got started on the wrong foot."

"Oh, what do you know about it, Jessica?" Lila shot back as she stomped into the bathroom and slammed the door shut.

Jessica sighed. At least she had tried. Obviously, Lila was never going to accept Bambi. It was a shame, too, Jessica thought. Bambi seemed perfectly nice, and she did amazing things with eyeliner.

Jessica went to her suitcase and retrieved the telephone number of the ski lodge where her family was staying. She had promised to call as soon as she arrived, and she knew they would be very worried if she forgot.

As Jessica picked up the receiver of the phone by her bed, she felt very grateful to have parents who made up all kinds of annoying rules for her to follow. From what she had seen today of Lila and her dad, she was beginning to think being spoiled wasn't all it was cracked up to be.

"Isn't this the most gorgeous beach you've ever seen?" Lila said later that afternoon, pointing to a lifeguard stand near the ocean's edge.

"Boy, you don't waste any time, Lila!" Mandy exclaimed.

Janet lowered her sunglasses to get a better view of the lifeguard. "Give it up, Lila," she advised her cousin. "He's way too old for you."

"That's what you said about the frozen yogurt guy at the mall," Lila reminded Janet. "You can't take all the guys just because you're older, Janet."

"The yogurt guy wasn't interested in *any* of us," Mary pointed out. "Even though we bought gallons of frozen yogurt!"

"Well, where do we start exploring?" Jessica asked, gazing at the long row of hotels and shops lining the beach.

"I think maybe I'll get a little sun," Lila said, her eyes still glued to the lifeguard stand.

"We can get sun in California," Mandy reminded her. "I want to go shopping."

"Didn't you hear my father's warning about tourist traps?" Lila asked. "They're total rip-offs, Mandy."

"But I *love* touristy junk shops!" Mandy protested.

"I was hoping to find some cute clothing stores," Janet said.

"Me, too," Ellen agreed.

"I've *got* to get some genuine Hawaiian clothes!" Jessica chimed in. "Plus, I promised to send Lizzie a postcard."

"Why don't we all go shopping at some of the tourist places first?" Mandy suggested.

"Actually, I was kind of hoping to watch some surfing," Mary said. "The guidebook says this area gets some amazing waves, and I can see some surfers down the beach."

"Cute *male* surfers?" Mandy teased.

Mary's gray eyes glittered. "I can dream, can't I?"

Jessica sighed. "Lila wants to lie on the beach, Mary wants to watch surfers, Mandy wants to go junk shopping, and Ellen and Janet and I want to buy clothes. We're never going to agree on anything!"

"Let's take a vote," Janet directed in her bossy, president-of-the-Unicorns voice.

"But you'll win!" Mandy protested.

"So?" Janet responded. "You know what Mrs. Arnette says. It's democracy in action."

"I've got an even better idea than democracy," Ellen said. "Why don't we each do what we want to do?"

"Why, Ellen, you've actually had your first good idea!" Lila said. "I guess even *you* have your moments!"

"We'll all meet back at the hotel by six," Janet instructed. "That gives us the whole afternoon to get to know Hawaii!"

"Lila?" Jessica called as Lila began heading off across the sand toward the lifeguard stand. "Where are you going?"

"To get to know Hawaii!" Lila replied with a grin.

# *Seven*

◇

Lila sauntered down the beach and scanned the sand for just the right spot. She had come prepared for some serious beach action. She was wearing her favorite purple bathing suit under a purple-striped coverup, and her beach bag was stuffed with all the essentials—sunscreen, a big beach towel, and a book to pretend to read while she checked out the scene. Lila smiled to herself. She knew that sightseeing in Hawaii really meant boy-watching.

The lifeguard stand was directly ahead of her. It was tall, wooden, and painted blue, with a little ladder on the side for the lifeguard to climb. The lifeguard in the chair had blond hair and a deep tan, and he was wearing a pair of red swim trunks and red sunglasses.

Lila examined the nearby competition before deciding on a spot in which to settle. Most of the sunbathers were young kids, although two older girls, probably high school age, were lying side by side near the base of the lifeguard stand. Lila decided to station herself directly in front of him, near the water's edge.

She spread out her towel and lay down, making sure to check the lifeguard every few minutes for signs of interest. *He's staring right at me,* she thought at one point, until she realized he was actually watching a young boy on a boogie board riding the waves behind her.

Lila had just decided to apply some sunscreen to her arms when a little boy trying to catch a Frisbee dashed right across her towel, leaving a trail of sandy footprints.

"Hey, you rotten little brat!" Lila shouted. "Do that again, and I'll drown you!"

Suddenly she realized that the lifeguard might not have appreciated her choice of words. She looked up at him and flashed a brilliant smile. "I have a way with children," she called to him.

The lifeguard stared straight ahead, stone-faced.

Lila sighed. He obviously did not have much of a sense of humor, but she was willing to overlook that teensy little fault. She brushed off her towel and lay back, closing her eyes. The warmth of the sun soothed her, and she began to relax. She had been a big bundle of nerves for the past couple of days. Bambi's presence at Fowler Crest had bothered her more than she liked to admit. Her father had never had a serious girlfriend before—certainly not one he had cared about enough to invite home for Christmas dinner. And every time Bambi had tried to be nice, it had only made Lila feel worse. Lila *knew* Bambi was trying to get on her good side. And she also knew the reason. Bambi wanted to hold on to Mr. Fowler, and she knew she could not get very far without Lila's approval.

Lila sighed and rolled over onto her stomach. The lifeguard was still staring out to sea. Had he even moved? *Maybe he's just a decoy lifeguard*, Lila thought.

Lila closed her eyes again and recalled Jessica's remark about how nice Bambi seemed. Jessica was so naïve! She came from one of those perfect families like the ones in all the TV sitcoms, with a mother and father and cute kids and a dog. All The Wakefields lacked was the dog!

Lila's life was different from the life of anyone else she knew. Sure, plenty of her friends had divorced parents. But none of them lived with their father. And Mr. Fowler was different from other fathers. For one thing, he was rich, which was great. But he also traveled all the time in order to *stay* rich, and that wasn't so great. Sometimes Lila's only real companion in the house was Eva, their housekeeper. Eva signed Lila's report cards, and made Lila's dinner, and did all those parental things Mr. Fowler would have done if he were home.

But it wasn't really so bad, Lila thought. She

was used to things being the way they were, just Lila and her father and Eva. *And there's no room for anyone else*, she thought angrily.

Lila opened her eyes. The lifeguard shifted his position slightly. Well, he was definitely alive. Lila sat up and cleared her throat. "You know, I think I just saw a jellyfish out there," she remarked loudly.

The lifeguard nodded his head slightly.

"I may have seen a shark, too," Lila added.

"I wouldn't joke about a thing like that," the lifeguard retorted.

*This guy needs to lighten up*, Lila thought grumpily. Maybe she should check out the next lifeguard stand a little way down the beach.

Lila began to gather up her belongings, when something in the sand caught her eye. It was a deep red color, in a shape too odd to be a shell.

It was a ring! She examined it closely, brushing off the grains of sand embedded in the elaborate carving. The ring was made of red stone, carved with what looked like the image of a Hawaiian god. It was strange-looking, even a little spooky, but Lila fell in love with it instantly.

*Someone important probably lost this ring*, Lila thought excitedly. She imagined an archaeologist frantically digging through the sand to recover this ancient—and extremely valuable—artifact.

For a brief moment Lila considered turning the ring in somewhere. A museum, or maybe an antique dealer, would probably pay a fat reward for something so rare. But as soon as she slipped the ring on her finger, she knew she could never part with it.

Just then, she remembered the lifeguard. Had he seen her find the ring? She sneaked a peek at him. As usual, he was staring at the ocean, his face blank. For once Lila was glad he wasn't paying any attention to her He might have made her turn it in to the police.

Lila reached for her beach bag and stood. " 'Bye," she said to the lifeguard. "It's been great chatting with you!"

She headed off in the direction of the next lifeguard station. As the beach curved away, the waves seemed to grow larger, and Lila saw a group of spectators watching some surfers. On the edge of the crowd, she noticed Mary sitting next to a girl with a long dark braid down her back.

"Mary!" Lila called.

Mary motioned for Lila to join her. "This is Mei," Mary said. "She's lived in this area all her life, and she's been telling me all about surfing."

"I've been telling her all about surfers, too!" Mei said with a laugh.

"Nice to meet you. I'm Lila. Sorry I have to drag Mary off like this, but—"

"But I just got here!" Mary protested.

"Mary, this is very important," Lila insisted. "And very private," she added in a whisper.

Reluctantly, Mary stood. "This better be good, Lila." She smiled at Mei. "I'll be back in a minute."

When Lila and Mary were a safe distance from the crowd, Lila decided it was all right to show Mary her discovery. "You're not going to believe my luck, Mary!" she exclaimed.

"Does this have anything to do with that lifeguard?" Mary asked impatiently.

"He wasn't my type," Lila said dismissively. She extended her hand. "Look at this ring I found in the sand. I'm sure it's some kind of ancient artifact."

Mary leaned close. "Weird," she commented.

"*Weird?*" Lila repeated. "That's the best you can do?"

"I mean, it's a good kind of weird," Mary said quickly. "But Lila, you can't keep it, you know."

"Of course I can keep it." Lila fingered the ring possessively.

Mary put her hands on her hips. "You should turn it in to the front desk at the hotel," she suggested. "They probably have a lost and found, and it's only fair to try to find the ring's rightful owner."

Lila hesitated. All she had wanted was for Mary to admire her new discovery. She had not expected her to have such a *conscience.*

She held out her hand. The ring looked perfect on her. "Even if I turned the ring in to the hotel, there's no guarantee that the person who lost it is staying there. This ring could have been lost months ago, even years! Besides, haven't you ever heard the law about finders, keepers?"

"That's not a law, Lila."

"It is where I come from." As far as she was concerned, it was her fate to have found this ring. Maybe it was a lucky omen that the trip was going to turn out better than she had hoped—Bambi and all.

That afternoon, Jessica, Ellen, and Janet returned to the hotel to try on the colorful T-shirts they had just bought. After that, Janet decided to go out to the beach and explore.

Janet took off her shoes and walked down to the ocean's edge, letting the cool water foam around her feet. She was reaching down to pick up a pretty pink shell when she noticed a group of four boys watching her from a few feet away. They were all cute, but one in particular made her heart jump as she met his eyes.

The boy was tall and slender and tan. His eyes were jet-black, and he was wearing faded shorts and a T-shirt with holes.

He smiled, said something to the other guys he was with, then began walking straight toward her. Janet stood and glanced over her shoulder, just to make sure he wasn't looking at some other girl.

"Hi," the boy said as he got near her. "I'm Kenji."

"I'm Janet," Janet replied, feeling her cheeks start to burn.

Kenji shook his head. "I don't think so," he said.

Janet narrowed her eyes. "What do you mean, you don't think so?" she asked warily.

Kenji's expression grew serious. "Come," he said, gesturing toward the sand, "sit down and I'll explain."

Janet hesitated. The guy was awfully cute. But what if he was awfully nuts, too?

She checked the area around her. There were plenty of people nearby in case it turned out she was in the company of a lunatic and had to scream for help. "OK," she said at last, settling beside Kenji on the warm sand.

Kenji stared at Janet for a long time, and she felt her face grow even hotter. "It's amazing," he murmured. "A miracle." He shook his head. "I apologize. It's just that for me to be the lucky one to find you—it's too much to be believed. At last, you have come back, Keiko!"

"Look," Janet said, starting to rise, "my name is Janet, not Keiko—"

"But you are the exact image of the beautiful princess Keiko!" Kenji exclaimed.

Janet paused. "Did you say *beautiful* princess?"

Kenji nodded. "Please don't go. I'll tell you the story of the princess."

Janet hesitated. The guy was probably crazy. Still, this would make a great story to tell the Unicorns. Her first day in Hawaii, and someone had actually mistaken her for a princess! A *beautiful* princess!

She sat back down. "OK," she said. "Let's hear it."

"It's a sad story, really," Kenji began. "A tragic one that all who live on our islands know by heart. As you know, long ago, Hawaii was ruled by kings."

Janet nodded, even though she hadn't known. History was not her best subject.

"There was a beautiful princess, Keiko, who was adored by all her people. She fell in love with a simple fisherman's son, and her father, the king, forbade her to marry the boy."

"But why?" Janet asked.

Kenji shrugged. "I guess he wouldn't let her marry beneath her class. Anyway, Keiko decided to run away with the boy. They were never seen again, and it was assumed that the young couple drowned at sea in the boy's tiny fishing boat. All the people of the islands grieved, and even Pele erupted in anger."

"Pele?"

"The volcano goddess," Kenji explained. "She is very powerful. And when she's *huhu*, watch out!"

"Did you say *huhu*?"

"That's Hawaiian. It means angry."

Janet frowned. "I don't get it. Why would you think I'm Keiko?"

"You are beautiful enough to be," Kenji said,

smiling shyly. "And"—he paused for a minute, staring at Janet intently—"you have a tiny beauty mark near your mouth, just as Keiko did."

Janet smiled. This was getting very interesting.

"Legend has it that Keiko will someday return to her homeland," Kenji continued. "Once she does, if she ever tries to leave again, Pele will unleash her fury"—Kenji's black eyes grew wide, and his voice rose—"consuming the islands in lava and burying all who dwell here." He paused. "Including Keiko."

"Bummer," Janet said, shaking her head. She tried to imagine the beach covered with molten lava, but it was hard to picture.

On the other hand, it was easy to see how she could be princess material. She was certainly beautiful enough. And hadn't she always been the most important girl at Sweet Valley Middle School? It made perfect sense. She had royal blood. No wonder she was president of the Unicorns! And no wonder she loved to wear purple, the color of royalty.

"Kenji," she said as she stood. "I'm awfully glad I ran into you!"

"No," Kenji said. "It is I who am honored." He stood, then bowed—just like in the movies, Janet thought. "Princess Keiko," he said, "welcome home."

# *Eight*

"Janet! Where've you been?" Jessica cried when Janet returned to the hotel room late that afternoon.

"My name," Janet announced, "is not Janet."

Lila and Ellen, who were lying on the bed painting their nails with a soft pink polish, both rolled their eyes.

"Since when?" Jessica demanded.

Janet waltzed across the room and examined her reflection in the mirror. "Since this afternoon. My *real* name is Keiko."

Jessica giggled. "How do you spell that? Is it like *cake*, with an 'o' on the end?"

"Have you ever noticed this little beauty mark by the corner of my mouth?" Janet asked, ignoring Jessica's remark.

"Don't worry about it," Lila advised. "I think you can have those things surgically removed."

"It is not a *thing*," Janet replied. "It's a *beauty*

*mark*. And it proves that I'm a real Hawaiian princess."

Mandy looked up from the postcard she was writing. "I think you've been out in the sun too long, Janet."

Janet whirled around. "I'm telling you guys the *truth*! I met this Hawaiian boy on the beach who recognized me right away as Keiko, the long-lost princess of the islands."

Mary burst into laughter. "Oh, please, Janet!" she cried.

"It's *true*!" Janet protested. "Princess Keiko disappeared with her true love, and all the islanders mourned, and a volcano goddess got really ticked off. . . ." Her voice trailed off as she surveyed the room. Jessica was trying on her new T-shirt, Lila was searching for some nail-polish remover, and Mandy and Mary were busy writing their postcards. Only Ellen seemed vaguely interested.

"Come on, Ellen," Janet said. "Let's go into the other room, and I'll tell you the rest of the story. Too bad no one *else* will get to hear it."

"I know *I'm* heartbroken," Mandy said with a laugh.

As Janet led Ellen through the doorway that connected the two rooms, Lila called out, "Hey, Janet! If you're a princess, does that make *me* royalty, too?"

"Of course not," Janet answered. "The legend didn't say anything about *cousins*, Lila!"

Lila turned her attention back to her nails.

"Oh, well," she said. "I figured it was worth a shot."

Janet closed the door behind her and sat down next to Ellen on one of the beds. "I left out the most shocking part of this whole story," she whispered.

"This is already pretty shocking," Ellen said. She paused to blow on her nails. "I mean, a Unicorn from Sweet Valley turns out to be a princess from Hawaii. . . ." She shook her head. "Of course, you *have* always had a sort of royal *attitude* about you, Janet."

"Attitude?" Janet asked, feeling pleased.

"You know. You're kind of bossy."

Janet decided to overlook Ellen's comment. After all, Ellen was the only one in the group who seemed even the tiniest bit interested in her story. "Well, anyway, let me tell you the rest of the legend. It seems that when Keiko returns to the island, she has to stay forever. If she tries to leave again, Pele—that's the volcano goddess—will erupt."

Ellen looked at Janet blankly. "So?"

"So? *So?* She'll cover all the islands with lava, Ellen, and everyone will die!" Janet paused for effect. Even as she retold the story, she got goose bumps. "Everyone!"

Ellen's expression clouded. "But the rest of us could leave, right?" she asked at last. "I mean, we could fly away while you stayed behind and got buried in lava, couldn't we?"

Janet sighed. All of a sudden she wasn't so

thrilled about her discovery. She had been so excited about being a princess that she had overlooked the part about being stuck in Hawaii forever.

Hawaii was nice, but it was no Sweet Valley.

"Why is there so much silverware?" Jessica whispered to Mandy at dinner Wednesday evening.

Mandy shrugged. "Search me. In case you're a real klutz and keep dropping things on the floor?"

"Isn't this place gorgeous?" Bambi exclaimed. "I could really get used to living it up this way!"

"I just bet you could," Lila muttered.

"This is almost as elegant as the cafeteria at school!" Mandy joked.

Everything in the hotel restaurant seemed to sparkle, from the chandeliers to the crystal vases on each table, filled with roses. Waiters in black tuxedos swooped across the room, carrying gleaming trays piled high with food on the tips of their fingers. In one corner, a quartet of musicians played classical music.

"I highly recommend the escargots," Mr. Fowler said, as everyone studied the menu.

"Sounds good. What is it?" Jessica asked.

"Snails," Lila answered haughtily. "You really should try them."

"I don't need to *try* them," Jessica replied, curling her lip in disgust. "I've *seen* them, and that was bad enough!"

"Well, order whatever you like," Mr. Fowler advised.

The meal was wonderful, and nobody wanted to leave when dinner was over—except Lila, who stood abruptly. "May I be excused?" she asked her father.

"Certainly," Mr. Fowler answered. He smiled at the rest of the group. "You can all go ahead, if you're through." He gave Bambi's hand a squeeze. "We'll stay here awhile longer and finish our coffee."

After they said their thank-yous, the girls left the restaurant and headed for the glass elevator in the center of the lobby. Lila led the way, her arms crossed over her chest.

"Did you see the way she acts with him?" she growled, punching the "up" button again and again.

"You mean Bambi?" Mary asked. "I didn't notice anything."

"Me, either," Jessica said.

"It was just nauseating!" Lila cried. "They were so lovey-dovey, I could have thrown up!"

"I don't know what the big deal is, Lila," Janet said dismissively. "That's how my mom and dad act."

Suddenly, no one said a word. The elevator arrived, and the doors opened slowly, but everyone was looking at Lila, who had a strange, sickly look on her face.

"Bambi is not and never *will* be my mother,"

she said in a barely audible whisper. "Do you all understand?"

Slowly, the group got onto the elevator. Just before the doors closed, Mandy stuck out her hand to stop them. "My purse!" she cried. "I must have left it in the restaurant!"

Mary reached over and pushed the "open" button, and the doors eased open again. "I'm going to go get it," Mandy said.

"I'll go with you," Mary said quickly.

The two girls dashed off toward the restaurant. "I don't know about you, but I was glad to get out of that elevator!" Mary said to Mandy. "I've never seen Lila so upset—and that's saying something!"

"Me, either," Mandy agreed. "I think she should give Bambi more of a chance. She seems kind of nice." She paused at the entrance to the restaurant. "I hope I didn't lose my purse. It's my favorite. I bought it at an antique store in Sweet Valley for fifty cents!"

"May I help you, ladies?" asked the maître d'.

"I think I left my purse at that table back there," Mandy said. "Do you mind if we take a look?"

"Be my guest," he said.

The table was at the rear of the restaurant behind a low brick wall. As they approached, Mandy and Mary could see the backs of Mr. Fowler and Bambi. They were sitting very close together.

Mandy paused a few feet from the wall. "I think he's got his arm around her," she whispered.

"I hope we're not interrupting anything," Mary whispered back, giggling softly.

"What if they're being—you know, romantic?"

"You could ask the waiter to look for your purse," Mary suggested.

Mandy glanced over her shoulder, but there was no waiter in sight. Suddenly Bambi's voice was clearly audible.

"The problem," Bambi said anxiously, her voice rising, "is that I don't have a maternal bone in my body. I'm so afraid I won't make much of a mother!"

"Of *course* you will," Mr. Fowler responded. "You can do anything you put your mind to!" He leaned over and gave her cheek a kiss.

Mandy looked at Mary in horror. "Oh, no!" she said in a hoarse whisper. "Lila's about to have a new stepmother!"

"May I be of some assistance, ladies?" came a smooth male voice.

Both girls leaped, and Mandy let out a startled cry.

"We were just, uh, just—" Mary babbled. She pointed to Mandy. "Her purse."

Mr. Fowler turned around and peered over the planter. "Forget something, girls?" he asked, smiling pleasantly.

"My purse," Mandy said, her cheeks flaming.

Bambi checked the seat next to her. "Here it is, Mandy. Safe and sound!" She admired the old beaded satchel. "This is darling," she said.

"I found it at an antique store," Mandy said, approaching the table to take it from Bambi's outstretched hand.

"I love shopping for antiques," Bambi said. "Maybe we girls can get together and go antique hunting when we get back to Sweet Valley."

"Sure," Mandy said quickly. "That would be great." She took a few steps backward and ran straight into Mary. "Well, good night."

"Is anything wrong, girls?" Mr. Fowler inquired. "You look a little flushed."

"Wrong? Nothing's wrong," Mary replied quickly. " 'Night!"

Mary and Mandy hurried from the restaurant. In the safety of the lobby, they came to an abrupt halt. "I wish we'd never heard that," Mandy said breathlessly. "*Now* what are we going to do?"

"You mean, should we tell Lila?" Mary asked. "Not if we want to live."

"It's really Mr. Fowler's place to tell Lila he's going to marry Bambi," Mandy pointed out.

"And we could be wrong," Mary said hopefully. "After all, there's no engagement ring."

"Good point," Mandy agreed. "Still, Bambi did talk about taking us antique shopping in Sweet Valley. That sounds like she's planning to be around for a while. And Lila *is* our friend. If I were her, I'd want to know." She sighed guiltily.

"Why don't we wait a bit before telling her?" Mary suggested at last. "Try to get some more information."

Mandy sighed with relief. *When in doubt, do nothing*, she thought. Now, that was a good plan!

# *Nine*

The next morning the telephone rang early, awakening Lila with a start.

"Miss *who*?" Lila asked drowsily, rubbing her eyes. "Oh, you must mean Jessica." She covered the receiver with her hand. "Jess," she called to the lump under the blanket on the other bed. "Someone calling for a 'Miss Wakely.' I guess they mean you."

"I'm sure it's a wrong number," Jessica growled, burrowing under her sheets.

Lila tossed a pillow at Jessica's head. "*Answer* it, will you?"

Reluctantly, Jessica roused herself and reached for the phone. "Hello?" she said hoarsely.

A few minutes later, she hung up the phone, now fully awake and smiling brightly. "Guess where we're going today?" she asked.

Ellen and Lila were both hiding under their

pillows. "I said," she repeated loudly, "guess where we're going?"

"Back to sleep," Lila growled. "That's where *I'm* going, anyway."

"Wrong." Jessica bounced onto the bed between Lila and Ellen. "Wake up, Lila, or I'll tell everyone that you kept me up all night with your snoring."

Lila sat up and glared at Jessica. "How many times do I have to tell you? I do *not* snore!"

"Whatever you say, Lila," Jessica replied. "That was the Pineapple People Company. Their headquarters is here in Maui, and they were calling to remind me that I'm supposed to visit them today for recipe-tasting and a tour of their plant. You're all invited. I've been so excited since we got here, I completely forgot about it!"

"What recipe will we be tasting?" Ellen asked sleepily.

"Mine and Mandy's, of course," Jessica said. She pointed to Lila's hand. "Hey, where'd you get the ring?"

Lila hesitated. "I got it while you were out shopping for postcards yesterday."

"It looks old," Jessica said, peering at the carving. "I like it."

"Too bad it's one of a kind," Lila said with a smug smile.

"I see you're still wearing the charm bracelet Bambi gave you," Jessica noted.

Lila pouted. "Daddy told me I have to wear it all during vacation so Bambi will know I appreciate it."

"Hey—when we go to visit those pineapple guys, you don't actually expect us to eat that glop of yours, do you?" Ellen asked.

"That's *prize-winning* glop," Jessica said indignantly, but the truth was, she had no intention of eating it, either.

The Pineapple People's main headquarters was a sprawling complex of low buildings. As soon as the girls arrived, they were ushered through the lobby, which was filled with pictures of pineapples being harvested. A woman led the group to a small meeting room, where they were asked to wait.

"I feel like a celebrity," Jessica whispered to Janet.

"If they knew I was Princess Keiko, they wouldn't care at all about you," Janet said haughtily.

"This is so exciting!" Bambi said, patting Jessica on the shoulder. "I wish George could have come along. It's a shame he had another business meeting this morning."

"That's OK," Jessica said, grinning at Mandy. "We'll save him a sample of our recipe!"

Just then, three men and a woman entered the meeting room. "Aloha!" said one of the men. "I'm Mr. Hakulani, vice-president of the Pineapple People Company. Which one of you is Miss, uh"—he glanced down at a clipboard he was carrying—"Wakely?"

Jessica raised her hand. "Actually, it's—"

"We're honored to have you here, Miss Wakely," Mr. Hakulani interrupted. "You and all your friends. We here at the Pineapple People Company are delighted you could visit our beautiful state. Where is it you're from?" He glanced down at his clipboard again.

"Sweet Valley," Jessica answered. "In California."

"Another beautiful state!" Mr. Hakulani exclaimed. "And how are you enjoying your visit so far?"

"It's been great!" Jessica said, and all the Unicorns nodded in agreement.

"We've got some wonderful things planned for you girls," Mr. Hakulani said. "First, a fascinating movie called *Pineapple Panorama*. It'll tell you everything you ever wanted to know about pineapple harvesting. It's in black and white—I'm afraid the movie's a bit old—but you're going to love it."

"I'll bet," Mandy whispered to Jessica. "Sounds like one of those boring movies they're always making us watch in social studies."

"After the movie," Mr. Hakulani continued, "I will personally take you on a tour of our ultramodern pineapple-processing plant. You'll see it all—crushed pineapple, sliced pineapple, pineapple chunks. And if you're really lucky, maybe I'll give you a glimpse of our pineapple juice operation!"

"I can't wait," Jessica said in an artificially bright voice.

"How long is the movie?" Mandy asked.

"Oh, about forty-five minutes," Mr. Hakulani answered.

"Oh," Mandy said, looking disappointed. "And how long is the tour?"

"Two hours, give or take fifteen minutes."

Mandy groaned. "I'm starving," she whispered to Jessica. "I hope we get something to eat besides the Poisonous Potato Salad!"

"Well, I hope you're all hungry," Mr. Hakulani said excitedly when the movie and tour were finally over. He led the group back to the meeting room where he had first welcomed them. When they entered the room, three other employees who were waiting there left through a side door. "This is going to be quite a treat for your taste buds, Ms. Wakely! It's a favorite with all of us here." Mr. Hakulani rubbed his large belly with his hand. "It's *ono ono*—that's Hawaiian for extra delicious!"

Jessica smiled awkwardly and exchanged a glance with Mandy. "Our Poisonous Potato Salad—*ono ono*?" Jessica whispered.

"Steven ate it," Mandy pointed out.

"Believe me, that doesn't prove a thing."

There was something else that was bothering

Jessica. Why did everyone here insist on calling her Miss Wakely? A nagging suspicion was beginning to form in her mind, but she tried to ignore it.

The three employees reappeared, pushing a metal cart on which sat a huge cake. The cake was decorated with yellow and white frosting, which formed the shape of pineapples around the edges.

"But that's a cake!" Mandy cried.

"Pineapple upside-down cake," Mr. Hakulani confirmed.

"Where's your green glop?" Lila whispered to Jessica.

Jessica shrugged. There was definitely something wrong here.

"Now, I want you all to help yourselves," Mr. Hakulani continued happily. "And when you're finished, we have complimentary cans of delicious Pineapple People crushed pineapple for each of you!"

Jessica nudged Mandy. "Come on. I'm going to the bathroom."

"But I'm starving!" Mandy protested.

Jessica gave her another nudge and headed for the door. "We'll be right back," she told Bambi.

Jessica marched to the ladies' room they had passed on their way in, with Mandy on her heels. Once inside, she slumped against a wall. "This doesn't make any sense, Mandy," she said with a sigh.

"You're telling me! What happened to our

glop? And why do they keep calling you Miss Wakely?" Mandy bit her lower lip. "Are you thinking what I'm thinking?"

"They made a mistake," Jessica said quietly. "Somewhere out there, somebody named Jessica Wakely thinks her beautiful pineapple-upside down cake lost the contest. *She* should be here, not me! Everybody *knows* I can't cook!"

"Should we tell the Pineapple People?" Mandy asked doubtfully.

"We could," Jessica said slowly. "But there's a good chance they'd put us on the next plane and send us home! I feel terrible now, but if we all had to go home, I'd feel even worse."

"*Much* worse," Mandy agreed.

Jessica squared her shoulders and took a deep breath. "I guess we'll just have to make the best of it. Promise you won't tell a soul?"

"Promise." Mandy paused at the bathroom door. "Jess?" she asked. "Do you feel as guilty as I do?"

"Guiltier," Jessica answered. "I feel so bad, I don't even want any cake!"

Back in the meeting room, Mr. Hakulani was trying to give Bambi one of the last pieces of cake. Bambi refused with a smile. "We girls have to watch our weight, after all!" she said.

Lila, who was already on her third piece, dropped her plate into a trash can and glared at Bambi.

Jessica poked Mandy and pointed to Janet,

who had just cornered Mr. Hakulani as he was biting into a piece of cake. "Mr. Hakulooloo?" Janet asked.

"Haku*lani*," he corrected.

"Are you a real Hawaiian?"

He nodded. "I was born right here on Maui."

Janet eased a bit closer, her head tilted awkwardly to one side. "Do I look *familiar* to you?" she asked hopefully.

"Familiar?" Mr. Hakulani asked. "Why, no. I'm sure we've never met."

Janet inched closer. "How about *this*?" she demanded, pointing to the tiny mole by her mouth.

Mr. Hakulani looked around helplessly. "This?" he repeated.

"My beauty mark. Doesn't it remind you of anyone? Anyone special?"

Mr. Hakulani frowned. "Well, my grandmother had a mole like that," he said at last. "She had it removed, though."

"Oh, never mind," Janet answered huffily and stomped off.

When everyone had finished eating, Mr. Hakulani passed out cans of pineapple, along with little plastic pins of a Pineapple Person with a smiling face.

Jessica put on her pin reluctantly. Every time she looked at it, she thought of poor Jessica Wakely, wherever she was.

\*　　\*　　\*

After dinner that night the Unicorns went for a walk along the beach with Bambi and Mr. Fowler. Later, they took a quick swim in the hotel's indoor pool before heading for bed.

"Hey, look at this!" Jessica exclaimed as she opened the door to the room. "Chocolate mints on our pillows again!"

"The maids leave them *every* night," Lila explained patiently.

"I love the candy," Mandy said, sinking into a chair with a sigh. "But my favorite thing about staying in a hotel is leaving the room a total disaster area and coming back to find it perfectly neat. I wish it worked that way at my house!"

A little while later, Bambi knocked at the door. She came in wearing her white hotel robe. "Just wanted to tuck you guys in," she said with a grin.

"Bambi!" Lila groaned.

"She's just kidding, Lila," Jessica said.

"We're going to leave for the volcano tour tomorrow morning at nine sharp, so don't stay up all night giggling," Bambi warned.

"Yes, Mom," Jessica teased.

"Hey, I kind of like the sound of that!" Bambi said with a laugh.

Mandy looked over at Mary uneasily. Was Bambi trying to drop a subtle hint?

When Bambi left and the girls began to settle down, Mandy realized she was keeping two secrets—the awful one about Mr. Fowler and

Bambi, and the awful one about the Pineapple People's mistake. It wasn't fair. All she had wanted to do on this trip was shop for souvenirs, and now here she was in possession of as many secrets as an international spy! She could only hope things didn't get any worse.

"Help me! Help me!" Jessica cried. "I'm drowning!"

"Jessica? Jess, wake up!"

Jessica's eyes flew open. Lila was standing over her. It was still dark outside. "I—I just had the most horrible nightmare," she said, sitting up slowly.

Lila sat down on the bed. "I was having one, too!" she exclaimed. "In fact, if you hadn't screamed just now, I'd probably *still* be having one!"

"I was drowning," Jessica said with a shiver. "But I wasn't in water." She paused and closed her eyes, trying to catch hold of the fragments of the dream before they drifted away. "I was in an ocean of crushed pineapple!"

Ellen giggled in the dark. "You could have at least made it an ocean of chocolate, Jessica!"

"This isn't funny, Ellen!" Jessica cried. "I couldn't breathe, and it was *horrible!*"

"You think that's bad?" Lila asked. "*I* dreamed I was at school, and I was on trial for stealing a valuable artifact. The court was in the cafeteria, and the principal was the judge. Every time he went to bang his gavel, it turned into a corn dog."

Ellen giggled again, but Jessica was too fresh from her own terrible dream to see any humor in Lila's. "Then what happened?" Jessica prompted.

Lila nervously twisted the red ring around her finger. "All I know is that when the next issue of the *Sixers* came out, the headline read " 'Unicorn Found Guilty!' "

"How come you guys are up?"

It was Janet, who eased open the door between the two rooms and tiptoed in. "How come *you're* up?" Ellen asked.

Janet sat down on the edge of Ellen's bed. "I had a nightmare," she said.

"Oh, brother!" Ellen groaned. "I dare you to try to top those two!"

"It was so weird," Janet said as she combed her touseled hair with her fingers. "I was eating this big sundae, and all of a sudden the chocolate syrup turned into bright red lava! The sundae just exploded, and there was lava everywhere—in my hair, on my crown . . ."

"Your crown?" Jessica repeated.

"A diamond tiara, like they wear in Miss America pageants."

Ellen jumped out of bed and grabbed her pillow. "Janet, do you mind if I sleep in your bed for the rest of the night?" she asked.

"Why?"

"Because you three definitely deserve each

other, and I intend to get a good night's sleep."
She shook her head and cast them a pitying look.
"I don't know what you guys ate at that Japanese
steak house, but do me a favor and don't ever
order it again. It definitely doesn't agree with
you!"

# Ten

◇

"How come you're so sleepy?" Mandy asked Lila on Friday morning as the volcano tour was beginning.

Lila yawned. "It's a long story, Mandy," she said. "Let's just say I didn't get much sleep last night."

"Girls!" Bambi called. "This way to the Visitors' Center." She pointed toward a small wooden building not far from the lot where Mr. Fowler had parked the Mercedes he had rented for the week.

Janet looked up at the mountain looming above them. "This sure is one big volcano," she said. "We don't have to climb the whole thing, do we?"

"I think they drive us part of the way up," Lila replied. "At least, I *hope* so. I'm way too tired to walk it."

"I'll bet you're glad your dad could come

today," Jessica said. "He's been so busy in the past couple of days, we haven't seen much of him."

"What do you mean by that?" Lila demanded. *Just because my father works harder than other fathers doesn't mean he isn't being a good father*, Lila thought defensively. Still, it was true that she *hadn't* seen much of him yet. But that was Bambi's fault, not his.

"I didn't mean anything, Lila," Jessica protested. "Really."

Lila smiled at Jessica. "That's OK, Jess," she said. She hadn't meant to be so grouchy to her friends. It was just that no one really seemed to understand her feelings about Bambi. The Unicorns actually seemed to *like* her.

The girls met up with Mr. Fowler and Bambi at the Visitors' Center, where several other tourists were already waiting. A woman in a green ranger's uniform stepped up to the group and smiled.

"Aloha, everyone!" she said brightly. "I'm Ranger Nani Kehena and I'll be taking you on your tour of Haleakala today—the world's largest dormant volcano. Dormant, by the way, means it's not active, so you've got nothing to worry about!"

"That's a relief, after my dream last night!" Janet whispered to Lila.

The group boarded a tour bus, and the ranger stood at the front with a microphone, pointing out features of the volcano as the bus slowly climbed it. "All the Hawaiian islands were formed by volcanic eruptions," she explained. "Haleakala was formed by lava we call *pahoehoe*. It's the hottest natural substance known on earth. Any questions so far?"

Mandy waved her hand. "Do they have any souvenirs back at the Visitors' Center?" she asked.

The ranger laughed and went on with her speech.

"I was *serious*," Mandy whispered to Lila.

When they neared the rim of the huge crater, the bus stopped in a parking lot. The group followed the ranger along a winding trail as she pointed out features of the terrain.

"According to legend, Pele is the volcano goddess," Ranger Kehena explained. "And when she's angry, watch out! That's when volcanic eruptions occur." She pointed out a rock formation. "We call hardened lava drops *Pele's tears*."

"Pele! That's my goddess!" Janet told Lila and Jessica. "The one who'll erupt if I ever leave the island!"

"Get a life, Janet," Jessica said impatiently.

Janet ignored Jessica's remark and stooped to pick up a glassy black rock on the ground. "How's this for a souvenir, Mandy?" she asked, slipping the rock into her pocket. "A piece of the volcano!"

Ranger Kehena smiled. "Some people say that Pele thinks of those rocks as her children.

When tourists take one, to Pele it's like kidnapping." She shrugged. "It's just part of island mythology, of course. But they say that taking one of Pele's children means bad luck for the kidnapper."

Janet reached into her pocket and dropped the smooth lava rock onto the ground. "I know all *about* Pele," she said nervously. "And I'm not about to annoy her if I can help it!"

Mandy trained her camera on the rock. "I'll take a picture of it for you, Janet," she said. "That's almost as good."

The group continued up the rocky slope. The ranger explained about the rare plants and animals that made their home on Haleakala, but Lila and Janet began to grow bored with the tour and hung back a bit from the rest of the group. "If I wanted a science lecture, I could have waited for Mr. Seigel's class!" Janet whined. "I hope we get to go shopping this afternoon."

" 'Fraid not." Lila shook her head sadly. "We're supposed to go on a glass-bottom boat tour. It was Bambi's idea, of course. I *was* hoping to spend the afternoon alone with my dad."

"Great. More science lectures. Who wants to look at a bunch of fish?" She glanced at Lila and pointed to the ring on her left hand. "Where'd you get the ring?"

Lila wanted to brag about her great find, but ever since her strange dream the night before, she had been feeling particularly guilty about the ring. "It's no big deal," she said vaguely. "I got it the other day."

"Let me see," Janet insisted.

Lila stopped walking and held up her hand so Janet could get a better look at the ring.

"Weird carving," Janet said, leaning close.

Lila suddenly gasped. "Oh, no!"

"What's wrong?"

"That stupid bracelet Bambi gave me for Christmas!" Lila cried in annoyance. "It's gone! I know I had it on in the car on the way over, so I must have lost it on the trail somewhere."

"So? Good riddance. It didn't go with any of your *real* jewelry, anyway."

"Daddy will kill me if he finds out. He made me promise to wear it around Bambi even though I told him I hated it. He'll think I lost it on purpose." She crossed her arms over her chest. "It probably fell off because the clasp on it was so cheap."

Up ahead, the tour group was nearly out of view behind a stand of small trees. "C'mon, Lila. We'd better hurry," Janet urged.

"We can always catch up to them," Lila said dismissively. "There's only one trail, and besides, that ranger lady stops to talk about some stupid rock every ten seconds." She spun around and began walking back down the trail. "I'm sure my bracelet fell off back there somewhere. Remember when we climbed over that big black lava rock? I'll bet that's where I lost it."

"Oh, well," Janet said. She sighed. "That tour was boring me anyway."

For several minutes the girls walked briskly, their eyes glued to the ground. Then they came to a sudden fork in the path. "I don't remember this part," Janet said. "Do you?"

Lila wiped her brow. "Nope. It sure is getting hot, isn't it?"

Janet nodded. "I'm dying of thirst. Too bad there's not a refreshment stand around here somewhere. They'd make a fortune."

"Which way should we go?" Lila asked.

"Search me. How about to the right?"

They veered onto the right path and kept walking. With every step the heat seemed to grow more intense. "I'm burning up!" Janet complained. "Why did it get so hot all of a sudden?"

Lila shook her head. "I don't know, but it's awfully strange." She scanned the path ahead of them. "Any sign of that big rock?"

"I don't even see any footprints, Lila," Janet said nervously, pointing to the path. "Maybe we should turn around. I'm getting a creepy feeling about this place."

"No," Lila said adamantly, although she was feeling anxious herself. "We know that stupid bracelet's not back there. Let's go just a little farther, OK?"

"Five more minutes, then that's it," Janet said bossily.

"It's *my* bracelet," Lila pointed out. "How come you get to decide when we give up?"

"Because I'm older, because I'm president of the Unicorns, and because I'm a Hawaiian princess," Janet said, tossing her glossy dark hair over her shoulders. "Take your pick."

Walking side by side, the girls continued down the path. "You know, it *never* gets this hot in California," Janet said quietly, wiping perspiration off her upper lip.

"If it weren't for Bambi and her cheap bracelet, we wouldn't be trudging around in one-hundred-and-fifty-degree heat, getting lost," Lila grumbled.

"Who says we're lost?" Janet said. "*I'll* say when we're lost, Lila."

The girls paused again and surveyed the stark rocky landscape. "OK," Janet said at last. "We are now officially lost."

Suddenly a low rumble met their ears. "Wait a minute," Lila said, grabbing Janet's arm. "Did you hear something strange just now?"

"I was hoping that was your stomach."

The rumble grew louder, like distant thunder coming closer. "That ranger lady said this volcano was dormant, right?" Janet yelled over the noise.

Before Lila could answer, the ground began to shake beneath their feet. "It's erupting!" she screamed. "We're going to be buried alive in lava!"

"What'll we *do?*" Janet cried.

"You're the princess. You tell me!"

The rumbling grew louder. "Pele!" Janet cried. "It's me, Princess Keiko! Mellow out, would you?"

As if in answer, the ground shook even more ferociously.

"A lot of pull *you* have!" Lila cried. "What's Plan B?"

"Run!" Janet shouted at the top of her lungs. "*Fast!*"

As the heat and noise grew more and more intense, the girls ran down the path, their hearts hammering in their chests. The path took a sudden sharp turn to the right, and they followed it blindly, hoping somehow for salvation.

Lila felt as if her lungs were burning. She had seen movies about volcanoes, so she knew that their only hope was to outrun the fiery rivers of molten lava that would cascade down the side of the volcano. She just hoped her legs would hold out. Suddenly she was grateful for all those laps Ms. Langberg had forced them to run in gym class.

The path changed and grew flat and hard, almost like blacktop. *Already the lava's beginning to harden,* Lila thought to herself. Then she heard a voice, a familiar, faraway voice—

"Smile!"

She stopped in her tracks. There before her stood a group of tourists carrying cameras, one of them focused on Lila and Janet.

"That's Mandy!" Janet cried. "It's our tour group!"

"How can you snap pictures at a time like this?" Lila demanded breathlessly. "The volcano's about to erupt!"

"Did I hear you right?" Ranger Kehena asked.

"The heat!" Lila said.

"And the shaking ground!" Janet added.

The ranger laughed. "It *does* get terribly hot here on Maui," she admitted. "But that heat comes from the sun. It was hidden by clouds on our way up the trail. When it reappeared, it got a bit warmer."

"But the rumbling—" Lila began meekly.

The ranger pointed to the far end of the parking lot, where a large bulldozer was rumbling away. "That's probably what you noticed," she explained. "They're enlarging the parking lot, and those bulldozers *do* make an awful lot of noise."

Lila and Janet looked at each other sheepishly.

"Don't worry about it," Ranger Kehena said kindly. "Volcanoes are strange places. They scare everybody a little bit, even when they're inactive." She looked over at the rest of the Unicorns, who were still laughing uproariously. "Hey," Ranger Kehena told them, "anybody could have made the same mistake."

Somehow, that was small consolation for Lila and Janet.

# *Eleven*

◇

"Do we have to go on this boat tour?" Lila complained that afternoon after lunch.

Mr. Fowler smiled. "It's not just *any* boat, Lila," he said. "It's a glass-bottom boat. You'll be able to see all kinds of sea life."

"You mean *fish*," Lila pouted. "You've seen one fish, you've seen them all, Daddy."

"It'll be educational," Mr. Fowler coaxed.

Jessica groaned softly. She was in complete agreement with Lila. Everyone knew that *educational* meant boring.

"Besides," Mr. Fowler continued, "Bambi and I want to do some shopping." He squeezed Bambi's hand. "Some *jewelry* shopping."

Jessica noticed Mandy and Mary whispering and wondered what they were saying. *They're probably discussing how mad Lila will be about missing out on a trip to a jewelry store*, she thought.

"Now here are your tickets," Mr. Fowler said,

passing one to each of the Unicorns. "The tour lasts two hours. Bambi and I will be waiting here to pick you up when the boat docks."

"Can't I go with you?" Lila pleaded.

"Not this time, honey," Mr. Fowler said. "But I promise to bring you something special, OK?"

Lila watched her father stroll off with Bambi on his arm. "It's not fair," she complained to Jessica. "I *love* shopping for jewelry! And anyway, what does Bambi know about jewelry? She bought me that hideous charm bracelet!"

Jessica glanced down at Lila's wrist. "Hey, where is your bracelet, anyway?"

Lila put her finger to her lips. "Shh! I lost it on the volcano."

"I hope Pele likes bracelets," Jessica joked. "At least you still have your Pineapple Person pin."

"How come you're not wearing yours?" Lila asked.

"It didn't go with my outfit," Jessica replied casually. The truth was, she couldn't bear to look at that pin. Every time she did, she remembered that she really didn't deserve to be in Hawaii. Jessica *Wakely* did.

Jessica nudged Lila toward the pier. "Come on," she urged. "You're about to learn everything you ever wanted to know about fish!"

"I know they come baked, fried, or stuffed," Lila said, hands on her hips. "And as far as I'm concerned, that's all I'll ever *need* to know."

"Well, it *is* going to be hard to top our last tour," Jessica remarked, "what with the volcano erupting and everything!"

Lila shot Jessica a withering look, but Jessica just smiled.

"All aboard!" cried a small man on the boat.

One by one, the girls stepped down into the boat. They sat down in a circle, while the man stood in the middle, a bamboo stick in one hand. But no one was interested in the man or in the captain, who was sitting in the raised cabin at the front of the boat. They were all staring at the floor, which was a solid sheet of glass.

"Wonderful, isn't it?" asked the man with the stick. His skin was weathered brown, and he wore a sailor's cap on his head. "My name is Palani, and I'm going to be your guide today on a wonderful excursion into the world of the sea."

"You've seen one fish—" Lila began.

"You haven't seen them all!" Palani finished with a good-natured laugh. "When's the last time you saw a red-lipped parrotfish? Or a blue-spotted cowfish?" He tapped the glass bottom with his stick. "Normally these fish are hidden from our view, but not on this boat! Keep your eyes on the floor, and as we pass things of interest, I'll point them out with my stick."

*A red-lipped parrotfish?* Jessica thought. Maybe this tour wasn't going to be so dull after all!

Next to her, Janet was making friends with two young boys, who were taking the tour with their grandmother. "Are you from Hawaii?" she asked the smaller boy, who looked to Jessica to be about six years old.

"Yes, ma'am," he said seriously.

"Do I look familiar to you?" Janet asked.

"Not again, Janet!" Jessica groaned.

"Have you ever seen me before?" Janet continued, smiling regally at the little boy.

"No, ma'am," he said quietly.

"Well, have you ever seen one of *these* before?" Janet asked, pointing to her mole.

The little boy's lips began to quiver, and suddenly he burst into tears.

"Stop poking your mole at people, Janet," Lila said crossly. "You're scaring them."

As the boat began to move, the little boy crawled into his grandmother's arms, staring at Janet and sniffling softly.

"I only thought—" Janet began.

"We *know* what you thought, Janet," Jessica said, rolling her eyes.

The wind was cool as the boat moved slowly away from the dock. Beneath them, the water bubbled and churned. It was crowded on Jessica's side of the boat, and she decided to move to the other side.

She stood up and took a step. Suddenly Jessica felt her right foot slip, and she flew into the air.

"No!" was all she had time to cry before she felt the water closing in around her.

She had fallen in! Jessica thrashed wildly. Her wet clothes and running shoes were pulling her down like anchors. She flashed back to her horrible nightmare. It was coming true, right before her eyes!

*Why isn't someone trying to save me?* Jessica wondered frantically. *Could the water be filled with sharks?*

She thrashed and bobbed and struggled for air, but it was no use. She was going to drown, right here in Hawaii! Some vacation this had turned out to be!

A muffled noise met her ears. Could it be voices she was hearing?

They were yelling something from the boat, that much she could tell. *Piranhas!* Was that what they were trying to tell her? That she was about to be consumed by a girl-eating fish?

The voices were clearer now. *"Your feet!"* someone yelled.

Jessica tried to kick her feet. Were they still there, or had the piranhas gotten them already?

"Put your feet down!"

It was Lila's voice, Jessica was sure of it. *My feet?* Jessica thought.

"There's only three feet of water!" Lila cried.

*Three feet?* How could she be drowning in only three feet of water?

Jessica eased her foot down. It hit something soft and yielding. She reached down with her right hand and scooped up a handful of sand.

Slowly Jessica stood upright, her hair dripping in her eyes, her wet clothes clinging to her. On the tour boat, the Unicorns were laughing so hard that the boat was slowly rocking back and forth.

"It's a red-faced Jessfish!" Mary exclaimed.

Slowly, with Palani's aid, Jessica climbed back into the boat. She was so humiliated that for a moment she considered jumping back in and hiding with the cowfish.

"How was the tour? Did you see any interesting fish?" Mr. Fowler asked when the girls met him on the dock a couple of hours later.

"Well," Mandy answered, barely hiding her smile, "there was this really big fish with blond hair and purple shorts."

"It's not funny, Mandy!" Jessica protested.

"Jessica!" Bambi exclaimed with concern. "Did something happen? You look a little . . . damp."

"I nearly drowned, is all," Jessica sulked.

"In three feet of water, no less!" Lila added, giggling. Lila turned to her father. "Did you buy me anything?" she asked eagerly.

"Sure did." He handed Lila a small brown-paper bag. "I bought Bambi a little something, too," he added.

"Look, everybody!" Bambi exclaimed. She held out her right hand. "George bought me the most beautiful pearl ring!"

As the rest of the girls crowded around to see Bambi's ring, Mandy hung back with Mary. "See?" she hissed. "What did I tell you? An engagement ring!"

"Wait'll Lila sees it!" Mary warned.

But Lila didn't seem impressed by Bambi's ring. She took a quick look at the pearl and shrugged. "I have lots of pearl jewelry," Lila said dismissively. "Bigger pearls, too." She looked up at her father, an excited smile on her face. "So what did you buy *me*?"

"Open it and see."

Lila ripped open the bag and tossed it to the ground. Inside was a box containing a small pink necklace. "It's coral," Mr. Fowler explained. "Do you like it, honey?"

Lila glanced over at Bambi, who was proudly displaying her ring to the others. "She gets a pearl, and I get some measly coral?" she demanded.

"But that necklace was quite expensive, Lila," Mr. Fowler replied.

Lila did not answer. She crumpled the necklace in her hand and brushed away a tear. Then she ran toward the parking lot where Mr. Fowler's rental car was parked.

As the others followed Lila, Mandy and Mary hung behind. "Do you really think that was an engagement ring?" Mary asked anxiously. "I thought they were usually diamonds. Besides, she was wearing it on her right hand, not her left."

"I suppose we could be wrong," Mandy said. "There's no point in getting Lila all upset for no good reason."

"Not in the mood *she's* in," Mary agreed.

"We need more proof," Mandy decided. "I'm not going to risk my life telling Lila about her father and Bambi unless I'm absolutely certain." She took a deep breath. "But I do think it's time to tell the others what we suspect, Mary."

"And then what?"

"Then," Mandy replied, "it's time for us to do a little detective work."

Lila stretched out on her beach towel and sighed. After they had all arrived back at the hotel, the other Unicorns had decided to go shopping, but she was in no mood to look at tacky trinkets. Her father had taken care of *that*, buying her that chintzy coral necklace.

Lila twisted her red stone ring around and around her finger. The truth was, she actually *liked* the necklace from her father. It would have looked perfect with her ring. But now, of course, she could never wear it. Not after seeing what he had bought Bambi.

It wasn't the ring she resented so much. Lila had lots of rings that were prettier than Bambi's. It was the fact that Bambi seemed to be becoming more and more a part of her father's life. But Lila still kept waiting for the day when she would wake up and Bambi would be gone.

*But what if she never leaves?* Lila thought anxiously. *What if Bambi is here to stay?*

"Mind if I join you?"

Lila lowered her sunglasses and blinked in the bright sunshine. There above her stood two incredibly cute Hawaiian boys, and they were actually talking to her!

"Sure," Lila said, struggling to sit up.

"I'm Kenji," said the taller boy, "and this is my friend Lono."

"Hi, I'm Lila. Are you from around here?"

"We live just up the road a bit," Kenji answered, his black eyes sparkling. "But we practically live on this beach!"

Lila glanced from boy to boy, trying to decide which one was cuter. Kenji had great eyes, she decided, but Lono had adorable dimples. It was a toss-up.

"Where are you from?" Lono asked shyly.

"California," Lila answered. "I'm just here for Christmas vacation. I came with a bunch of friends," she added with a flip of her hair. There was no point in mentioning that her father and his girlfriend had come,too.

Kenji picked up a handful of sand and let it flow through his fingers. "How do you like Hawaii so far?"

"It's OK," Lila said noncommittally. So far, this hadn't exactly been the vacation of her dreams.

"Just *OK*?" Lono asked in surprise.

"This is Hawaii!" Kenji exclaimed. "A tropical paradise! How can you just call it *OK?*"

"Well, if you'd been through what *I've* been through . . ." Lila said melodramatically.

Kenji's eyes went wide. "Tell us!" he implored.

Lila sighed. "Well, first of all, I haven't had a good night's sleep in *days.*"

"Too bad," Lono said sympathetically, shaking his head.

"And today I lost a very valuable bracelet," Lila said. "A priceless family heirloom," she added for effect. "And as if that weren't enough, I visited a volcano this morning, and it nearly erupted!"

Kenji gasped. "You must have been terrified!" he exclaimed.

Lila nodded and let out a long-suffering sigh. She was enjoying all this attention. So what if she was exaggerating a tiny bit?

"To top it all off," she said, her voice low, "my very best friend in the whole world nearly drowned this afternoon in a tragic boating accident!"

"Is she all right now?" Lono asked.

"Is who all right? Oh, you mean Jessica," Lila said. "Yes, she's fine. Although *I'm* still trying to get over the trauma."

Suddenly Kenji frowned. "Your ring!" he said harshly. "May I look at it?"

Lila held out her hand, and Kenji peered

closely. Without a word, he jumped to his feet, signaling Lono to do the same.

"We must go," Kenji said, his voice quavering with fear.

"But . . . but what's wrong?" Lila demanded. She was definitely not having good luck with the guys on this beach. "A minute ago, everything was fine!"

"A minute ago, I hadn't noticed your ring!" Kenji took a few steps backward. "Come on, Lono!" he urged. "Let's get out of here! Now, before it's too late!"

# Twelve

◇

"Wait!" Lila commanded, scrambling to her feet. "Tell me what's wrong, please!"

Kenji stopped in his tracks. He looked over at Lono. "I suppose we should tell her," he whispered loudly.

"But is it safe?" Lono demanded.

"We'll have to take that risk," Kenji decided. He returned to Lila and pointed to her ring. "There's a reason why you've been so unlucky," he told her. "It's because of your ring."

Lila felt her cheeks begin to flush as she recalled her horrible nightmare. Maybe she should have listened to Mary in the first place and turned the ring in.

"That ring," Kenji continued, "is no ordinary ring. It's the sacred burial ring of King Kamehameha!"

"You mean they buried this ring with a *dead* person?" Lila cried.

"Not just any dead person. King Kameha-meha. That's his face carved into the stone."

Lila held her hand up and examined the ring closely. "Not a good-looking guy," she commented.

"Perhaps not," Kenji said, "but he was a great warrior and ruler." He shook his head sadly. "By wearing that ring, you have violated a sacred Hawaiian tradition, and now you must pay the price."

"You don't really believe that stuff, do you?" Lila asked as she examined the ring again. But when she looked up, Kenji and Lono were dashing across the sand as fast as their legs could carry them.

*This is crazy*, Lila told herself. *A ring can't bring bad luck.* Still, watching the boys run away, she wasn't entirely convinced she was right. She thought of all the bad things that had happened recently, and she realized that she *had* been wearing the ring all along. Was it just a coincidence, or was it something more?

*Just in case Kenji is right*, she decided, *I'd better get rid of the ring.*

Lila pulled on the ring, but it wouldn't budge. She ran over to the ocean's edge and dipped her hand in, hoping the cold water would shrink her finger enough so that she could slide the ring off. She yanked and twisted and groaned, but the ring remained wedged on the fourth finger of her hand.

Lila frowned and stared at the red stone carving. Why hadn't she noticed how angry the face looked until now? It was hideous, really. How could she ever have admired it?

Just then, a young boy carrying a red and yellow surfboard walked past her. "Hey," Lila called plaintively, "could you give me a hand with something?"

The boy looked at Lila uncertaintly. "You talking to me?"

"Uh-huh." Lila nodded. "I need someone to help me get this ring off."

The boy set down his surfboard. "So what do you want me to do?"

Lila extended her hand. "Pull on it," she said, "as hard as you can."

The boy brushed a lock of black hair out of his eyes. "Well, OK, if you say so," he said reluctantly. "But don't blame me if your finger pops off."

Lila bit down on her lower lip as the boy grabbed hold of the ring and began to pull. He groaned and grunted, but even after several tries the ring hadn't moved at all. "Sorry," he said with an apologetic shrug. "I guess your finger's too fat."

"Thanks, anyway," Lila said sullenly, staring at her swollen finger.

The carved face of King Kamehameha looked back up at her and seemed to laugh.

"But I thought we were going shopping!"

Ellen protested as Mandy and Mary gathered the girls together on the balcony for a conference.

"We will, if there's time," Mandy said. "But first things first. We have to talk now while Lila's out on the beach." She took a deep breath. "Mary and I have some very important news. We think Lila's about to have a new stepmother."

Ellen gasped. *"Who?"*

Mary rolled her eyes. "Take a wild guess, Ellen!"

Ellen's face clouded.

"Bambi, Ellen!" Mandy exclaimed in exasperation. "Mr. Fowler's going to marry Bambi!"

*"Oh,"* Ellen said. "Why didn't you just say so?"

"But how do you know, Mandy?" Jessica asked.

"We don't—not for sure," Mandy admitted. "But we overheard Bambi talking about being afraid she wouldn't be a good mother. And Mr. Fowler bought her that ring today."

"That doesn't exactly prove anything," Janet pointed out.

Mandy nodded. "We know. That's why we haven't said anything up until now, particularly to Lila."

"Do you think Lila will call her Bambi, or just plain Mom?" Ellen asked thoughtfully.

"Could we stay on the subject, *please?*" Mandy continued. "Here's the plan. We all agree that before we talk to Lila, we need to get more proof. So first we're going to get one of the maids to open Bambi's room. Then, when she's not looking, we'll sneak inside. After the maid leaves, we'll search for clues."

"What kind of clues?" Jessica asked.

"Something that will tell us for sure that Mr. Fowler and Bambi are engaged," Mary answered. "A love letter, maybe. Or a bridal magazine."

"Sounds risky to me," Ellen said. "What if Bambi finds us in there?"

Mandy shook her head. "She went to have her hair done, remember? And her appointment's not for another half-hour. She won't be back for a long time."

"But how do we get a maid to open Bambi's door?" Janet asked.

"We've already thought of that. One of us has to call the housekeeping department and pretend to be Bambi," Mary answered.

"I don't get it," Jessica said.

"We'll complain that she needs more towels," Mandy explained. "They'll send a maid up to deliver the towels, and while she's in the bathroom, we'll sneak inside and hide."

Ellen sighed. "This is insane!"

"Yeah, but it sure sounds fun!" Jessica exclaimed. "And besides, we owe it to Lila to find out what's going on."

"Who wants to be Bambi?" Mandy asked. "How about you, Jess? You're a good actress."

Jessica stepped back into the room and dialed the number for housekeeping. "Quiet!" she warned. "No giggling, or you'll ruin everything!"

Then Jessica cleared her throat. "Hello? This is room number 1823, and I must say I was very disappointed in your maid service today. I don't have nearly enough towels!" she exclaimed. "What kind of towels?" Jessica looked at her friends and shrugged helplessly. "*I* don't know," she replied. "White towels."

Jessica paused a moment, then nodded. "All right, I'll be out having my hair done, but you can come up right away. Thank you."

She hung up the phone and smiled deviously. "Mission accomplished," she said. "Towels are on the way!"

"I'll be the lookout," Janet volunteered. She ran to the door and cracked it open an inch while the other girls waited behind her.

A few minutes later, Janet held up her hand to signal for silence. "The maid's here," she whispered, "with a ton of towels!"

"Is Bambi's door open?" Mary asked softly.

Janet nodded.

Mandy led the way into the hallway, where the group paused in front of Bambi's door. It was open a crack, and they looked in. There was no sign of the maid in the bedroom—which, they hoped, meant she was putting the towels in the bathroom.

Mandy eased open Bambi's door and dashed

across the room to the sliding-glass door that led to the balcony. The maid *was* in the bathroom, her back turned, placing towels on a rack and humming to herself.

The other girls followed Mandy, who gently unlocked the balcony door and slid it open. Then they slipped onto the balcony, one at a time, and Mandy closed the door behind them. Unless the maid looked closely, Mandy was sure she would never notice them through the sheer curtains.

Seconds passed, and the maid left the bathroom. A moment later, she closed the door to the room behind her.

"Whew!" Mandy exclaimed, as she slid the doors open and entered Bambi's bedroom. "That was close!"

"Let's hurry up and get out of here," Ellen said. "I'm afraid we're going to get caught."

"Relax, Ellen," Mary replied. "Bambi won't be back for another hour at least."

"So where do we start?" Jessica asked.

Mandy looked around helplessly. The room was neat, and except for Bambi's open suitcase on her bed and a novel on the night table next to her bed, it looked as if no one were staying there. Suddenly, Mandy felt a pang of guilt. They *were* invading Bambi's privacy by being in her room. "You guys, maybe this whole idea is silly," she said softly.

"But we just got here!" Jessica protested.

"Does anyone see anything?" Mary asked.

"Like what?" Janet inquired, her brows arched. "A bridal gown in the closet?"

"I don't know," Mary shrugged. "I'm starting to think maybe Mandy's right about this. I sort of feel guilty about snooping around in here."

"Me, too," Janet agreed. "Let's go, everybody."

"I'll just check the bathroom first," Jessica volunteered.

Ellen picked up a magazine on the dresser. "Look!" she said excitedly. "There's an article in here called 'How to Win Your Man'!"

"So?" Janet asked. "That doesn't prove anything, Ellen."

"Jessica?" Mandy called, heading toward the door. "Let's get out of here, OK?"

"You won't believe Bambi's eye-shadow collection!" Jessica yelled from the bathroom. "It's absolutely amazing!"

"Hurry up, Jess!" Mary urged.

"There's actually a shade here called Silver Unicorn!" Jessica exclaimed.

Ellen and Janet ran for the bathroom. "Let's see!" Ellen cried.

Mandy folded her arms over her chest. "We're *never* going to get out of here now," she groaned.

"I guess it's really our fault," Mary observed. "After all, you and I were the ones who came up with the brilliant—'' She stopped in midsentence, her eyes wide with fear. ''What was that?''

''The door!'' Mandy whispered. ''Run for cover!''

Mandy and Mary dashed for the balcony. Just as Mary pulled the sliding door shut behind them, Bambi entered the room.

''What about Jessica and Ellen and Janet?'' Mandy whispered.

''There's nothing we can do now,'' Mary said grimly. ''They're on their own.''

# *Thirteen*

◇

"Did you hear something?" Jessica whispered to Janet.

Janet gulped, nodding. "Like a door?"

"It's awfully quiet out there," Ellen said.

Jessica tiptoed to the bathroom door. From there, she could just make out two shadowy figures on the balcony, nearly hidden by the curtain.

She jerked back, her heart pounding wildly. "Either there's somebody breaking in on the balcony, or Mandy and Mary are hiding out there. In any case, we're in deep trouble!"

"Bambi's back?" Ellen whispered.

Jessica held her finger to her lips and peeked into the room. Bambi was sitting on the bed, her back to Jessica, dialing a number on the phone.

"She's calling someone!" Jessica reported in a barely audible whisper.

"How's her new hair style look?" Ellen asked.

Janet elbowed Ellen in the ribs. "Zip it up, Ellen."

"What are we going to do now?" Jessica asked. "What if she comes into the bathroom?"

"We could hide," Ellen suggested.

"Where? In the medicine cabinet?" Jessica said.

"How about the shower?" Janet said. "We could pull the curtain shut."

"That's just great, unless she decides to take a shower." Jessica chewed on her lower lip, trying to think clearly. "I know!" she exclaimed. "She can't take a shower if there aren't any towels."

"But there are *tons* of towels," Ellen pointed out. "Don't you remember? You called house-keeping."

Jessica gritted her teeth. "Yes, Ellen. The point is that now we have to *hide* them. Quickly." She peeked back outside. Bambi was still on the phone, but they probably didn't have much time.

"There's no place to hide anything," Janet complained.

"How about the toilet?" Ellen offered.

"Too gross." Jessica's eyes lit on the empty wastebasket. "Stuff them all in there, then cover the top with tissues so she won't notice. In the meantime, I'll keep an eye on Bambi."

Jessica peeked out the door. Bambi was still on the phone. "I know, Sid, I know," Jessica heard her say. "And believe me, I'm going to do the very best I can to make them happy."

Jessica turned back to Janet and Ellen. Ellen had a foot in the wastebasket as she tried to cram down more towels. "I think she's talking about getting married!" Jessica reported.

She eased her head back out the door again. "You really think I'll make a beautiful bride?" Bambi said now. "Let's just hope I get to *be* a bride, Sid. There's a lot of competition out there, and I don't have any experience."

Jessica's mouth dropped open. She pulled her head back into the bathroom. "You won't believe this!" she hissed.

"I don't believe *this!*" Janet grumbled, as she crumpled another piece of tissue and tossed it on top of the overflowing wastebasket.

"It sort of looks like a sno-cone," Ellen remarked, eyeing their handiwork. "You know, we could have just put the towels in the tub."

"It's a little late for that now, Ellen!" Janet groaned.

Suddenly, there was silence in the bedroom and the click of the receiver as Bambi replaced it in its cradle. "The tub!" Jessica whispered hoarsely. "Now, before it's too late!"

The three girls dived into the bathtub at the same time. Jessica and Janet landed directly on top of Ellen. "Get *off* of me!" Ellen whispered. Jessica and Janet ignored her and yanked the shower curtain shut.

" 'Here comes the bride,' " Bambi sang as she stepped into the bathroom.

Jessica huddled in the corner of the tub, trying not to breathe. Janet sat next to her, her face pale, while Ellen lay on the bottom of the tub.

There was a sound of running water in the sink, and then soft rattles as Bambi searched through her makeup case. "That's strange," Bambi murmured to herself. "No towels."

Jessica peered around the shower curtain. Bambi was combing her hair, and there was no sign that she had noticed the stuffed wastebasket yet. A moment later, Bambi spun around and left the bathroom.

"Boy, that was close!" Ellen whispered as she struggled to sit up. "Now what?"

"Now we wait," Jessica said softly, "until Mandy and Mary give us the all-clear."

"What if they're waiting for us to go get them?" Janet asked.

As if to answer the question, Mandy and Mary burst into the bathroom. Mandy pulled open the shower curtain and giggled. "Three to a shower!" she exclaimed to Mary. "Are you guys trying to conserve water?"

"Is she gone?" Jessica asked.

Mary nodded. "Let's get out of here while we still can. We thought you were goners for sure!"

The group dashed out of Bambi's room and across the hall to the safety of their own room. "That's the last time I spy with you guys," Jessica said crossly.

"Well, we wouldn't have been stuck in the bathroom to begin with if you hadn't insisted on checking out Bambi's makeup supply!" Ellen retorted.

"Did you hear Bambi's phone call?" Mandy asked.

Jessica nodded gravely.

"What did she say?" Janet asked. "We were busy stuffing towels in a wastebasket."

"She said she hopes she's a beautiful bride, but there's a lot of competition out there and she doesn't have any experience," Mary said.

"Then she came in the bathroom and sang 'Here Comes the Bride,' " Jessica added.

Mandy sighed. "Well, we've got our evidence," she said quietly.

"Now the big question is," Jessica added, "what do we do with it?"

"Look at this!" Janet said when the girls returned to their rooms after dinner. "No chocolate mints on the beds! The maids must have forgotten us!"

"I'm beginning to think one of us is jinxed," Mandy said crossly.

"What do you mean?" Janet asked as she casually browsed channels on the television with the remote control.

"Well, it seems as if things keep going wrong. There was the volcano incident with you and Lila—"

"That was a simple misunderstanding," Janet broke in defensively.

"And Jessica nearly drowning," Mandy added. "Then this afternoon—" Mandy looked over at Lila, then stopped abruptly.

"What about this afternoon?" Lila asked.

"I meant this evening," Mandy said quickly. "No mints on the beds." She shrugged. "You know what I mean. Little things."

Janet sighed. She really *was* jinxed, unlike the others. Ellen hadn't seemed overly impressed when she had heard the news, and there was no point in trying to convince everyone else of her fate. *They* could safely leave Hawaii. *She* couldn't. Now, recalling Kenji's words, Janet shuddered. She was beginning to wish she had never run into him on the beach and that she had never heard of Princess Keiko. A fat lot of good it did her to be a princess if it meant being a virtual prisoner!

Saturday morning, the Unicorns headed out to the beach together to lie in the sun. "At least we don't have to go on another fish tour!" Janet said.

"We're on our own *all day*," Lila said. "My dad's got another business meeting, and Bambi said she had something to work on. Whatever *that* means."

Janet looked over at Jessica and shrugged. Bambi was probably hunting for wedding invitations. Someone was going to have to break the news to Lila soon—and gently. Normally, Janet would assume that was her responsibility. After all, Lila was her cousin, and being president of the Unicorns meant Janet had certain social obligations. But ever since she had discovered her real identity, Janet didn't feel overly concerned about taking responsibility for her friends. Unicorn business seemed a little silly now, compared to the responsibilities and pressures of being a doomed princess.

Janet had just settled onto her beach towel when she realized that she was completely out of sunscreen.

"There's a little shop over there," Mandy said, pointing down the beach. "They sell every kind of suntan oil ever made. The other day I bought a bottle made with coconuts, bananas, and cherries."

Reluctantly, Janet reached for her wallet and stood. She hated to get up once she was nicely arranged on her beach towel for sunning. Positioning was *so* important.

When Janet got to the little store Mandy had described, though, it was almost worth getting up for. Just as Mandy had promised, it carried a complete supply of tanning products. Janet was browsing through the oils, trying to find the perfect combination of sunscreen and fruit ingredients, when she heard a familiar voice.

"Keiko!"

Janet whirled around to see Kenji standing in

the candy aisle. Next to him was another dark-haired boy, with big dimples.

"Hi, Kenji!" Janet said as she began to walk over to greet him.

"No, Princess!" Kenji held up his hand. "It is *I* who must come to greet you!" He dashed over to Janet's side, his dimpled friend right behind him.

Kenji got down on one knee and bowed to Janet. When his friend just stood there, Kenji gave him a swift hit in the shin. "Forgive my friend, Lono," Kenji apologized. "It has been so long since we have had a princess in our presence, we have forgotten our manners."

"Oh," Lono said, a smile dawning on his face, "the *princess!*" He sank to his knees.

A boy stocking groceries nearby turned to stare. "Amazing," he muttered. "Some guys will do *anything* to get a date!"

Janet wondered briefly about the meaning of the stockboy's comment, then shrugged.

"You may rise," Janet told Kenji and Lono. It was a relief to finally be around people who gave her the respect a doomed princess rightfully deserved!

"How does it feel to be back in your home-land?" Kenji asked, while Janet continued to search the shelves for suntan oil.

"Not bad, I guess," Janet said distractedly. She picked up a brown bottle. " 'Papaya and boysenberry with extra ultraviolet protection,' " she read. "Sounds good to me."

Kenji and Lono followed behind Janet while she made her purchase and headed outside. "You don't sound satisfied with your return to Hawaii," Kenji said worriedly. "Has anything happened?"

Janet sat down with the boys on a bench outside the store. "Well, you know," she said with a sigh. "Little things."

"Such as?" Lono pressed.

Janet thought back to the incident on the volcano. There was no point in admitting what fools she and Lila had been. Still, it would make a good story if she told it in the right way. "I was on Halea—" she began. "Halea—"

"Haleakala," Kenji finished for her. He smiled understandingly. "I'm sure your memory of these places will improve with time."

"Well, anyway, I was touring—um, *visiting*—the volcano, when it suddenly began to erupt."

Kenji and Lono both gasped. They were watching Janet so intently that she felt she should spice up the story a little more. "There was a huge river of lava coming straight at me, but I managed to outrun it."

"Thank goodness for that!" Lono exclaimed.

"And later," Janet continued excitedly, "I was on a boat, and—"

"Let me guess," Kenji interrupted. "Somebody fell out?"

"Worse!" Janet said, carried away with enthusiasm. "The *whole* boat capsized!"

"Incredible!" Lono said.

"Unbelievable!" Kenji agreed.

"Fortunately, we were all saved when I flagged down a fishing boat."

"It's a miracle you're still here with us," Kenji said. "To lose you so soon after finding you, Princess"—he paused and swallowed hard—"it would have been too much to bear!"

"Yes, I know," Janet said with a satisfied smile. She really was made for this princess line of work. Being adored came naturally to her.

Lono's face grew dark. "I fear that Pele was trying to send you a message," he said ominously.

"Next time, a simple phone call would do," Janet joked.

"Lono is serious, Princess," Kenji said. "You haven't considered leaving the island, have you?"

"Well, not exactly." Janet lied.

"Pele was trying to remind you that you must never leave here, or great tragedy will befall us all," Kenji explained.

"But what about the boat accident?" Janet asked. "Pele's the volcano goddess, not the tourboat goddess."

Kenji glanced at Lono. "But she has great power," he said at last.

"Yes!" Lono agreed quickly. "Great power. Power that goes far beyond volcanoes."

Kenji bowed once again. Lono did the same.

"We must be going now, Princess," Kenji explained. "I hope we meet again soon. Please do not forget what we have told you. Our lives depend on it."

"I won't," Janet said anxiously as she watched the boys depart. For a few minutes, she considered everything they had said to her.

Suddenly, she was struck with a terrible stab of homesickness. She wanted to see her mother and her father, and her brother, Joe, and her cat. She wanted to eat frozen yogurt at the mall and gossip at the Unicorner during lunch.

But she would never do any of those things again. Sweet Valley was no longer her home. She trudged slowly back to the Unicorns, carrying her papaya-boysenberry suntan oil. It was beginning to look as if she would need a lifetime supply of the stuff!

# Fourteen

◇

"What's that disgusting smell?" Jessica asked, rolling over onto her back.

"Janet's new suntan oil," Mandy answered, giggling. "Where have you been? We've been teasing her about it for an hour."

"I guess I fell asleep," Jessica said. "Being near the ocean always makes me sleepy."

"Well, it makes me hungry," Ellen said. "Anybody feel like lunch yet?"

"I do," Lila said. "But I want to go back to the hotel and change first." She examined her shoulders tenderly. "I think I'm starting to burn."

"Use some of Janet's sunscreen," Ellen suggested.

"No way!" Lila exclaimed. "She smells like rotten fruit."

"I think I'm going to stay here a while longer," Jessica said, closing her eyes. "I'll meet you back at the hotel."

"Don't forget we're going windsurfing this afternoon!" Mary reminded Jessica.

"How could I forget? You've been talking about it all morning," Jessica replied.

The others walked off, and Jessica started to doze again. Moments later, she was awakened when someone stepped on the edge of her towel.

"Oh, sorry," said a cute Hawaiian boy wearing cutoffs.

"He's such a klutz," said the boy's friend. Jessica noticed he had huge dimples when he smiled.

"I'm Kenji," said the first boy. "And this is my friend Lono."

Jessica sat up and flashed the boys one of her very best smiles. She couldn't believe her luck! Two boys all to herself, when only seconds ago all the Unicorns had been here! "I'm Jessica," she said. "Have a seat."

The boys plopped down in the sand. "Where are you from, Jessica?" Lono asked.

"Sweet Valley, California," she answered. "I'm here because I won a contest."

"I'll bet it was a beauty contest," Kenji said.

Jessica felt her cheeks heat with color. Lono was awfully cute, she decided, but Kenji definitely had a way with words! "Actually, I won a cooking contest."

"You can cook, too?" Kenji asked. "I think I'm in love!"

Jessica giggled. "It was a *national* contest. There were *thousands* of entrants."

"And how do you like our fair state?" Kenji asked.

"It's OK," Jessica answered vaguely.

"OK?" Lono cried indignantly. "Just OK?"

"Well, my vacation hasn't exactly gone as I'd planned," Jessica admitted.

"What do you mean?" Kenji asked, leaning toward her.

Jessica thought of all the terrible things that had happened since her arrival on the island. There was the mix-up with the Pineapple People, and the problem with Bambi and Mr. Fowler, but those were topics she didn't want to get into. "For one thing," she said, "there was the volcano incident."

"Are you talking about Haleakala?" Lono asked, his eyes wide.

Jessica nodded. "That's the one." She had planned to tell them about Janet and Lila making fools of themselves on the volcano tour, but the boys looked so interested, she decided she would dress up the story a little bit. "I was exploring the volcano with a friend," she began, "when suddenly the entire mountain seemed to shake, and red-hot lava came spurting out of the top!"

"No!" Lono cried.

"You must have been scared to death!" Kenji added.

"Yes—well, no. I didn't have time to be

afraid. The lava was pouring down the side, and I knew in moments I'd be buried alive."

"What did you do?" Kenji asked nervously.

"I dashed to the nearest tree," Jessica said breathlessly. She was really enjoying herself now. This was great practice for her acting career. "But my friend had fainted when the lava was only inches away from us. I had to carry her up to the top branches. Seconds later, we would both have been buried alive."

"What a story!" Kenji marveled. "It's a miracle the tree didn't burn down, isn't it? I mean, lava usually destroys everything in its path."

"Yes, well . . ." Jessica hesitated. "It was a very strong tree, I guess." She leaned back, basking in their admiration. "You'll never guess what happened later."

"Surprise me," Kenji urged.

"I was on a glass-bottom tour boat way out in the ocean, when suddenly the boat began to sink."

"Oh, no!" Lono exclaimed. "Not sharks, I hope!"

"Well, no," Jessica said. "As a matter of fact, it was a school of piranhas. They'd chewed right through the side of the boat." Jessica looked at the boys, whose eyes were wide with fear. She was a better actress than she had ever dreamed! These guys were eating it up!

"What did you do?" Kenji demanded.

"What anyone in my position would have

done," Jessica said humbly. "I saved the other passengers by pulling them to a life raft."

"But *you* could have been eaten alive!" Lono cried.

Jessica sighed. "Somebody had to do it. So you can see, I haven't exactly been having good luck since I got here."

Kenji was silent for a moment. "You know, Hawaiians have a saying," he said at last. "It goes, *Ua Mau Ke Ea O Ka Aina I Ka Pono*. And it means, 'The Life of the Land is Perpetuated in Righteousness.' "

Jessica yawned. She really didn't feel like a language lesson, even if it was from a cute guy. "So?" she asked.

"The point of the saying is that only those who are pure in heart are allowed to stay in Hawaii in peace. The island gods curse all those who are dishonest." Kenji eyed Jessica suspiciously. "Have you perhaps told a lie since arriving in Hawaii?"

Jessica hesitated. "You mean, like a white lie?"

"No"—Kenji shook his head—"a *big* lie."

"Of course not!" Jessica declared indignantly. *And even if I have, what business is it of yours?* she added silently. These guys were cute, but they were way too nosy for her taste. She stood abruptly and gathered up her towel.

"Remember what I told you," Kenji warned.

Jessica stomped off toward the hotel, but an annoying thought kept tugging at her conscience. What if she had offended the island gods by not telling the Pineapple People the truth the other day?

If only she could talk to Jessica Wakely, the real contest winner, she would tell her this whole vacation thing wasn't what it was cracked up to be.

Lila was in the hotel room examining her sunburned shoulders in front of the mirror when there was a knock at the door. "Would you get it, Ellen?" Lila asked.

"I can't," Ellen said. "My nails are wet."

"You just did your nails!"

"I'm putting little red stripes on them."

"Your mother doesn't let you wear red polish!" Lila snapped.

"My mother's not in Hawaii," Ellen replied with a sly grin.

Lila sighed and went to the door. "Bambi!" she exclaimed when she opened it. "I thought you were going to be gone all day."

"Mind if I come in?" Bambi asked.

*Yes*, Lila thought, but she shrugged and let her in.

"Hi, Ellen!" Bambi said. "Nice nails." She turned to Lila. "Actually, I'm going to be gone this afternoon," Bambi explained. "The hairdresser had to cancel my appointment yesterday, and nobody else could fit me in, so I've got to go back today."

Ellen began coughing loudly.

"You OK, Ellen?" Bambi asked.

"Nail polish fumes," Ellen explained, her face red.

"Anyway," Bambi continued, "I've been spending so much time cooped up in my room working on my upcoming audition that I'm dying to do a little shopping. I thought that maybe tomorrow you and I could spend some time together, hitting the boutiques. We really haven't had a chance to get to know each other the way I thought we would."

Lila looked down at the floor. She didn't *want* to get to know Bambi any better. She already knew everything she had to know—that Bambi was ruining her life. Still, if her father heard that she had refused to go shopping with Bambi, she would probably be in big trouble.

"If you've got other plans, I understand," Bambi said softly.

"No," Lila replied. "That'll be fine, Bambi."

"Great," Bambi said brightly. "Oh—" she said, reaching into her purse to retrieve a small piece of paper. "Here's the number of the hairdresser, in case you need me." She handed it to Lila as they walked to the door. "I'll see you guys tonight. Your dad said he's taking us on a dinner cruise."

"See you then," Lila said indifferently. She was just about to shut the door when Jessica appeared in the hallway.

"Hi, Bambi," Jessica said crossly.

"Anything wrong, Jess?" Bambi asked.

"Oh, you know. Just *guys*," Jessica replied. Bambi smiled and left. Jessica stomped into the room and dropped onto a bed.

"Hey!" Ellen complained as the mattress bounced. "You're ruining my nails!"

"What guys, Jessica?" Lila asked.

"They're not worth talking about," Jessica groaned, crossing her arms over her chest.

"Who aren't we talking about?" Janet asked, stepping through the doorway that connected the girls' rooms.

"We're not talking about guys," Lila explained.

"That's fine with me!" Janet said hotly. "The only guys I've met here so far have been nothing but trouble!"

"I'll second that!" Lila agreed. She thought of Kenji and Lono and looked down at the image on her ring. King Kamehameha was glaring at her with empty eye sockets. She was considering having her finger amputated just to get rid of him.

"Let's change the subject," Jessica suggested irritably. "What did Bambi want, Lila?"

"She wants to take me shopping," Lila said. "Probably to some discount store!" She slumped into a chair. "She says she wants to get to know me better."

Lila sighed. She was tired of thinking about Bambi. Tired of being angry at her, even. Soon this vacation would be over, and maybe then Bambi would be gone for good. "Fortunately, I won't have to put up with her too much longer," Lila added.

Nobody said a word. Lila looked around the room. Jessica, Ellen, and Janet were all staring at her intently.

"What is wrong with you guys?" Lila demanded.

"Ellen, go get Mandy and Mary," Janet instructed.

"But why?" Ellen whined. "All I have left to do is my pinkie finger!"

Janet glared at Ellen, and without another word of protest she jumped off the bed and ran next door.

"What's going on?" Lila asked, this time more forcefully. Something about her friends' serious expressions sent a chill down her spine.

"We need to talk, Lila," Jessica said gently.

Lila twisted her ring on her finger. "So talk."

Jessica looked up as Mandy and Mary entered. They, too, looked anxious.

"Did you tell her yet?" Mandy said.

"Tell me *what*?" Lila demanded.

Jessica cleared her throat. "There's a reason Bambi said she wants to get to know you better, Lila," she began. "She's going to be your new stepmother."

# Fifteen

Lila sat perfectly still. She did not say a word.

"Lila?" Mary said softly.

"Are you OK?" Jessica asked.

"Bambi will *never* be my stepmother," Lila said quietly. *"Never."*

"But we heard—" Mandy began.

"I don't *care* what you heard!" Lila cried. "I won't let it happen!"

"Lila, I don't think you have a choice," Mary said gently.

"Maybe it won't be so bad," Jessica offered. "Think of all the great makeup you can borrow."

"Yeah, look on the bright side," Janet suggested. "Your dad could have picked some old witch. At least Bambi's nice."

"And she's an actress," Mandy added. "That's something."

Lila stared at her friends in disbelief. *Nobody*

*understands!* she thought. *I don't want my world to change. I like it just the way it is!*

She got up and walked toward the door.

"Where are you going?" Jessica asked.

"To find my father," Lila answered.

"But why?" Mandy demanded.

"To tell him he can't marry Bambi," Lila said.

"You can't just *tell* him that," Janet protested.

"Why not? He's always done what I've wanted him to."

"But this is *different*, Lila," Jessica argued. "And besides, there's the chance things still might fall through."

"Fall through?" Lila echoed. "You mean, they might not get married?"

"Well, sure," Jessica replied. "These things often don't work out. I know from watching *Days of Turmoil.*"

Lila hesitated by the door, her hand still on the knob. "No," she said at last. "I have to tell Daddy how I feel."

"Come on, Lila," Mandy urged. "Just give it a little more time. Maybe this is just puppy love."

"Adults don't get puppy love."

"Sure they do," Ellen said. "All the time."

"I suppose you're right," Lila said reluctantly. And then she realized her friends must have known about Bambi and her father for some time. "Why didn't you tell me as soon as you knew about this?" Lila demanded angrily.

"We wanted to be absolutely sure first,"

Mandy replied. "We didn't want to ruin your whole vacation, Lila."

"Bambi's taken care of that already," Lila said wryly. She walked back to her chair and sank into it. "I guess I should take your advice about waiting," she admitted. "But it's going to be awfully hard to keep my mouth shut."

"We know!" Jessica said with a grin.

Lila looked at Jessica and felt the beginnings of a smile. "I'm really glad I have you guys, you know that?" she said softly.

"It's all going to work out OK, Lila," Jessica said. "You just wait and see."

With all her heart, Lila wanted to believe that Jessica was right. But with the way her luck had been going lately, she just couldn't do it.

Lila sulked all that afternoon. "I *told* you I didn't want to come windsurfing! Every time I try to stand up, I wipe out," she said.

"Me, too," Jessica agreed. "But it's a good way to take your mind off your troubles, Lila. Besides, Mary's friend Mei claims it gets easier once you learn how to control the board and catch the wind with the sail. She says it's easier than regular surfing."

Lila watched Mei float gracefully over the water on the crest of a wave. "She's probably been windsurfing since she was three," she said bitterly.

"Mary's doing a pretty good job," Janet

remarked. "At least she's actually managing to stay above the water. And Mandy's not so bad, either." She picked up a shell and tossed it into the waves. "I wonder why *we* keep wiping out."

"We're jinxed, that's why," Lila replied. She pulled on her ring, hoping that it might ease off this time. It wouldn't budge.

"It's your turn to use the windsurfer next, Lila," Jessica said.

"Be my guest," Lila replied. "I'm going to buy some serious sunscreen. My shoulders are killing me. It's just my luck that I'm the only one who got sunburned!"

Lila left her friends and headed for the little store down the beach. The truth was that she was less interested in finding sunscreen than she was in finding Kenji and Lono. The more she thought about everything that had gone wrong, the more she realized that she had to find a way to end the curse that was ruining her life. The news about Bambi and her father was the last straw. King Kamehameha was coming off her finger, no matter what.

As she wandered up the beach, she noticed a volleyball game in progress. The server looked awfully familiar. "Kenji!" she screamed, just as he was about to serve the ball.

Kenji turned in the direction of her voice, and the volleyball dropped to the ground.

"Sorry," Lila said after she had run over to join him. "But I really need to talk to you, Kenji."

Kenji groaned. "But we're ahead by two points!"

"*Please*," Lila begged. "It's urgent."

Kenji signaled to Lono, who came over to join them. The boys sat down with Lila on the warm sand.

Kenji eyed Lila's ring warily. "Make this quick," he said. "I don't want to be near you for too long. Not while you're wearing that ring."

"But that's why I'm here!" Lila cried. "The stupid ring won't come off my finger, and my luck is getting worse by the minute! How do I get rid of this curse, Kenji?"

Kenji frowned. He seemed to be deep in thought. "The ring will not come off until you go to the tomb of King Kamehameha," he said finally.

"OK," Lila said eagerly. "Where is it? I'll have my father drive me."

"Not so fast!" Lono exclaimed. "She has to go alone, doesn't she, Kenji?"

Kenji nodded. "Alone, and in the middle of the night. The tomb is deep within a cave that lies in an ancient forest."

Lila looked around nervously. Why couldn't the king have his tomb in a museum, like other sensible dead people? "How am I going to find this place?" she asked.

Lono shrugged. "Just ask any cab driver. They all know where it is."

"Oh," Lila said. "I guess that's easy enough."

"*Not* so easy." Kenji looked out at the ocean. "I'm sorry to tell you this, Lila. Many people have gone into the tomb of King Kamehameha, but nobody has ever come out."

Lila shuddered. Was it worth the risk, to be rid of all her bad luck, and maybe even of Bambi? "You're sure that when I get there the ring will come off all by itself?" she asked doubtfully.

Kenji stood and brushed sand off his knees. "Positive."

"Well, thanks, you guys," Lila said, staring down at the ring that was causing so much trouble in her life. "I'll think about what you said, even though it seems awfully dangerous."

"Not as dangerous as keeping the ring," Kenji warned.

"It's been nice knowing you, Lila," Lono called as the boys trotted back to their game.

It took Lila a minute to realize that it sounded as if Lono were saying goodbye for the last time.

"Janet! What happened to your head?" Lila asked when she returned a while later.

"Runaway Frisbee," Janet growled, gingerly rubbing the bump on her forehead.

Just then another Frisbee whizzed past her head. "Hey, learn to throw, would you?" she yelled. She jumped up and reached for her beach bag. "That does it," she said. "I'm going for a walk. It's safer than sitting here waiting to get killed."

"But it's your turn to windsurf!" Jessica said.

"That's OK. I'd probably only drown."

Janet didn't really have a destination in mind, but in the back of her mind she was hoping she would run into Kenji and Lono. Ever since they had told her that she was Princess Keiko, her luck had been getting worse and worse. She had decided to ask them how she could give up her throne and go back to Sweet Valley with her friends.

Fortunately, Janet found the two boys playing volleyball. "Kenji?" she called loudly, just as he was about to return a tough shot.

Kenji jerked around, and the ball dropped to the sand with a thud. "This better be good!" he growled, motioning to Lono.

"How can you talk to your princess that way?" Even though she was tired of being Princess Keiko, Janet still thought she deserved the respect of her subjects.

Kenji and Lono instantly dropped to their knees. "Forgive me, Princess!" Kenji cried. "You've been gone so long that your subjects have forgotten their manners!"

"OK. No big deal," Janet said. "Look, I came to see you because I've decided I can't go through with this princess thing. It was fun for a while, but I want to go back to being Janet now."

Kenji's jaw dropped open. "But—but you can't be serious!"

"Of course I'm serious. I've got a round-trip ticket, and I intend to use it."

Kenji looked at Lono, then again at Janet. "Please, Princess," he pleaded, "I beg you to spare your subjects!"

Janet sighed. "You mean that whole lava thing?"

"We will all perish for sure!" Lono moaned.

Janet tapped her foot impatiently. "Look," she said, "isn't there some way to bribe the Pele goddess? What if I gave her some kind of offering? You know, like a curling iron or something."

Kenji shook his head sadly. "Nothing will appease Pele but your presence in Hawaii. Forever."

Janet chewed nervously on her thumbnail. "What if I throw in a Johnny Buck cassette?"

"Please, Princess," Lono begged. "You must accept your true identity."

"There's really nothing I can do?"

"Nothing," Kenji answered. "I am truly sorry, Princess."

Janet stared at the two boys for a moment. Could it be she was really trapped in Hawaii forever?

When she felt hot tears begin to form, Janet turned and slowly walked away. Somehow, it didn't seem right to let her subjects see her cry.

"Jessica! What happened to your foot?" Janet asked when she returned.

"I stepped on a jellyfish," Jessica moaned, rubbing her throbbing foot.

"That little store might have something you could put on it," Mandy suggested "Do you want me to go check?"

"That's OK," Jessica said. "I'll go myself. You can have my turn on the windsurfer, Mandy. I've had all the fun I can stand for one day."

"Can you walk?" Lila asked.

Jessica took a tentative step. "I can hop," she answered. "See you in a while."

Jessica hobbled along the sand. Her foot burned like crazy, but that wasn't the real reason she had decided to go to the store. She was hoping to run into Kenji and Lono. She hated to admit it, but she was certain that all her bad luck was a result of not revealing the truth to the Pineapple People. But even if she wasn't totally pure of heart and mind, she was sure there would be a way to convince the angry island gods that she wasn't really such a bad person.

She spotted Kenji and Lono playing volleyball. "Kenji!" Jessica called, just as he was about to leap into the air to spike a ball over the net.

He twisted around when he heard her voice and landed on the ground with a thud. The ball dropped directly on his head.

"What's with you and the girlfriends, Kenji?" someone called. "You're ruining the game."

Kenji motioned for Lono and trudged over to Jessica. "What is it?" he asked.

"Sorry about the ball," Jessica said.

"That's OK," Lono replied. "He's used to it."

"Let me guess why you're here," Kenji said. "Is this about the bad luck you've been having because you told a lie?"

"Well, yes," Jessica began. "How did you—"

"Here's the deal," Kenji said quickly. "You must cleanse yourself in order to appease the gods."

"You mean, like take a shower?"

"No," Kenji said. "I mean you must follow an ancient recipe."

*Great,* Jessica thought. *More cooking. That's what got me into this mess in the first place.*

"By the light of a candle," Lono added.

"At midnight," Kenji said. "While wearing your hair in a ponytail on top of your head."

"A ponytail?" Jessica repeated. "Are you sure about that?"

"Absolutely," Kenji responded. He reached into the back pocket of his cutoffs and withdrew a small notepad and a stubby pencil. "I'll write down the recipe for you. Remember, you must follow it exactly."

"That's what Mrs. Gerhart's always telling me."

"What?" Kenji asked.

Jessica shrugged. "Long story."

"After you read this at midnight, you'll have exactly fifty-seven minutes to gather the ingredients, make the potion, and drink it. You must do this alone."

Kenji paused, consulted in whispers with

Lono, then wrote something on the piece of paper. He folded it into a tiny square and handed it back to Jessica.

"You're sure about this?" she asked, narrowing her eyes. "It sounds like a lot of work."

"The gods don't appreciate lying," Lono reminded her.

"Thanks, guys," Jessica said. "I'll think about it. Maybe I'll head over to the store and pick up a candle, just in case I decide to go through with it."

"Don't wait too long," Kenji warned. "And Jessica?"

"Yes?"

"One more thing. You'll never tell a lie again, will you?"

Jessica hesitated, then shook her head. "Never," she lied.

# *Sixteen*

◇

"Jessica, are you ready?" Lila asked impatiently. "Our dinner reservations are for seven-thirty, you know."

Jessica put her hand over the phone. "I'm calling the ski lodge one more time, Lila. Lizzie wasn't in when I called before."

"Well, hurry up," Lila said, pausing to admire herself in the mirror. "Daddy and Bambi and the rest of the Unicorns are downstairs in the lobby waiting for us."

"I'll meet you down there," Jessica said. The phone in the Wakefields' room at the ski lodge continued to ring.

The receiver still to her ear, Jessica picked up the smiling Pineapple Person pin and stared at it forlornly. She was just about to hang up when she heard Elizabeth's breathless voice at the other end.

"Lizzie?" Jessica said. "Is that you?"

"Jessica!" Elizabeth exclaimed. "I just walked in the door! I ran up to the room to put on an extra pair of socks, or I would have missed your call! Is something wrong? We just talked to you this morning."

"No," Jessica said hesitantly. Nothing was wrong, exactly. It was just that nothing was *right*. "I just felt like saying hi."

"What'd you do today?" Elizabeth asked. "More fun in the sun?"

"I windsurfed—sort of. Mostly I wiped out. And I stepped on a jellyfish. That was pretty much the highlight of my day."

"Jess, are you really OK?" Elizabeth asked.

"Yeah, I'm OK." Jessica sighed. "Tonight Mr. Fowler's taking us on a dinner cruise."

"Sounds great!"

"I guess." For a moment Jessica considered explaining to her twin why she couldn't really enjoy the cruise or anything else about the trip. The terrible deception she had perpetuated with the Pineapple People weighed too heavily on her conscience. But she couldn't bring herself to admit what she had done. Elizabeth was the kind of person who would have confessed to the Pineapple People right away. And then she probably would have sent Jessica Wakely, the pineapple upside-down-cake girl, a letter of apology.

"Jess? What's wrong?"

"Nothing's wrong."

"Are you sure?"

"Of course. What could be wrong?" Jessica asked sullenly. "I'm in a tropical paradise, Lizzie."

"Guess what I did today?" Elizabeth asked.

"What?"

"I made it all the way down the intermediate slope and only fell once!"

"Congratulations," Jessica said. "Well, I guess I should go." She hated to hang up. Talking to her twin made Jessica feel that everything was going to be OK.

"A floating restaurant!" Mr. Fowler exclaimed as the group took their seats at a table near a wide picture window. "Isn't this a great idea, honey?" He leaned toward Lila, who was sitting on his right. "Lila, honey?"

"Oh," she said sullenly. "Were you talking to me?"

"I said, isn't this a fine idea!" Mr. Fowler leaned back in his chair. "I must say, I'm honored to be in the company of such a lovely group of ladies."

Jessica unfolded her napkin and smiled at Mr. Fowler. He seemed to be loosening up more as the days went by, joking and laughing like her own father. Could that be because he was excited about his engagement to Bambi? Or was he just getting used to being around six middle-schoolers?

Lila, on the other hand, seemed tenser than ever. She was very quiet, carefully watching

Bambi and her father. Jessica hoped Lila would keep her promise and not say anything to her father that she would regret later.

"So, I hear you're quite the windsurfer, Mary," Mr. Fowler said as he glanced over his menu.

"She's the only one of us who didn't wipe out," Janet said.

"Beginner's luck," Mary said modestly, but Jessica could tell she was very proud of her performance. "I'm thinking of taking up surfing when I get back to Sweet Valley," Mary added.

Janet, who had been taking a sip of water, suddenly began to choke.

"Are you OK, Janet?" Bambi asked, as Janet coughed and spluttered.

"Yes," she finally managed to answer, her face red and her eyes watering. "Sorry." She wiped away a tear. "I don't know what came over me."

"Well," Mr. Fowler said, "I've got quite an appetite tonight. How about the rest of you?"

"I'm not very hungry," Lila said quietly.

"I'm not either, actually," Bambi agreed.

"You're probably just nervous about your audition," Mr. Fowler said.

"When *is* the audition?" Lila asked.

"Monday," Bambi said. "I'm flying back to Los Angeles Sunday evening."

"Good," Lila murmured.

"What was that?" Mr. Fowler asked sharply.

"I mean, *good luck*," Lila corrected herself.

"You're supposed to say *break a leg*," Mandy informed Lila. "It's bad luck to say good luck."

"Sorry," Lila said indifferently.

Janet leaned close to Jessica. "Where's the bathroom?" she whispered.

"That way, I think," Jessica said, pointing. "We passed it on the way in." She turned her attention back to Bambi. She loved hearing about acting, even if the person talking was someone who had never actually *acted*. "What are you trying out for, Bambi," Jessica asked.

"Well, I'd rather not say too much," Bambi said nervously. "I'm afraid I'll jinx myself if I talk about it—"

Just then Janet pushed back her chair to stand. At the same moment, a waitress walked by behind the chair, carrying a big oval tray piled high with food. Before anyone could warn Janet or the waitress, the tray went flying—and the waitress with it.

"Oh, I'm so sorry!" Janet gasped, dropping to her knees to help the waitress to her feet. "I just didn't see you!" Janet grabbed some French fries with one hand and a piece of fried fish with the other. "Here," she said frantically, handing them to the waitress.

"That's OK, really," the waitress said, backing away as if she were afraid of Janet. "I'll go get a busboy. There's no need for you to clean up." The waitress dashed off, while Janet remained kneeling on the carpet, surrounded by a pile of cole slaw and mashed potatoes.

"I really didn't see her," she said again apologetically.

"That's OK, Janet," Bambi said reassuringly. "We've all had embarrassing moments at one time or another."

"But we're having more than our share of them lately," Jessica said under her breath.

Once the floor was cleaned up and Janet had washed the mashed potatoes off her dress, the waitress brought the group their drinks and they considered what to order from the menu.

Lila was reaching for her soda when Mr. Fowler's eyes locked on her wrist. "Lila, what happened to the charm bracelet Bambi gave you?"

Lila continued gulping down her soda, as if she were trying to buy some extra time before answering.

"She doesn't have to wear it every minute of the day, George," Bambi protested.

Lila put down her empty glass. "I lost it on the volcano," she said, her voice almost defiant.

"Why didn't you say something before now?" Mr. Fowler asked angrily.

"It was just a little trinket," Bambi said quickly. "We can always get another one."

"Lila?" Mr. Fowler pressed. "What do you have to say for yourself?"

Jessica watched nervously as Lila hesitated. At last Lila opened her mouth to speak, but instead of the angry flurry of words that Jessica had been expecting, out came the loudest, most ear-splitting, window-rattling burp she had ever heard!

The entire room fell absolutely silent. People at other tables twisted in their seats to see who was responsible for such a repulsive sound. One little boy sitting nearby applauded.

"Lila!" Mr. Fowler's face turned red.

"I didn't mean to, Daddy," Lila cried. Her face was the color of the red rose in the center of the table. "Really I didn't. I guess I just drank too much soda."

Mr. Fowler sighed. "*I'll* say!"

Jessica was afraid to look at any of the other Unicorns, for fear she would break into uncontrollable laughter. She stared at her menu and chewed on her tongue. Between Lila's burp and Janet's knocking over the waitress, this meal was not going well at all.

For several moments the table was quiet. Everyone seemed afraid to open their mouths. Finally, Jessica decided to break the ice. "Bambi," she said pleasantly, "I couldn't help noticing that wonderful eye shadow you have on. What's it called?"

"Let me see," Bambi said. "I've got it right here with me." She reached into her purse and withdrew a tiny compact. "Here," she said, reaching behind Janet to hand Jessica the compact. "See for yourself."

Jessica leaned back in her chair to take the eye shadow from Bambi. Just as her hand fastened on the compact, she felt her chair begin to tip backward.

"Oh, no—" Jessica cried as her chair tipped all the way over and landed with a crash.

Jessica struggled to stand, picked up her chair, and sat down. A few muffled giggles met her ears. She looked down at the compact in her hand and tried to compose herself. " 'Silver Unicorn,' " she read brightly, pretending that nothing at all had happened. "What an interesting shade."

"That was the worst dinner of my life," Jessica cried as the Unicorns prepared for bed that night.

"Actually, I thought it was pretty entertaining," Mandy said. "It's a tough call which part was funniest, though—Janet sitting in a pile of cole slaw, Lila's mega-burp, or your chair gymnastics."

"Laugh all you want, Mandy," Jessica growled, "but *I* think we're all cursed."

"*Some* of us are, anyway," Janet agreed. She sat down on the bed and kicked off her shoes. "Maybe it's time we all just accepted our fate."

"You mean it's your fate to be a klutz?" Mandy teased.

Janet ignored Mandy. "I've been giving this a lot of thought, you guys," she said seriously, "and I've decided I want you to start calling me Princess Keiko."

"Janet!" Mary cried. "Not *that* again!"

"I'm *serious*," Janet insisted. "I also want you to start bowing in my presence."

"Don't hold your breath on that one, Janet," Jessica added. She wasn't in the mood for Janet's little fairy tale. Not tonight, when she was battling a guilty conscience.

Janet crossed her arms over her chest and surveyed the room. "Come on," she pleaded. "Didn't you hear me?"

Ellen stepped over and did a little curtsy. "Good night, Princess Keiko," she said dutifully.

Janet nodded with satisfaction. "I guess that's better than nothing," she said. She stood and headed for her room. " 'Night, everybody," she called. "You coming, Mandy and Mary?"

"Yes, Your Highness!" Mandy said, giggling.

When the girls had left, Jessica climbed into bed and stared at the ceiling. It was time to take action. She could see that now. Tonight's dinner had been the last straw. She was willing to try anything, even Kenji's recipe, to make her life go back to normal.

Jessica reached for her wallet on the nightstand and withdrew Kenji's recipe. Then she hid it under her blanket. "It's getting late," she said, glancing at her watch.

"Eleven forty-five," Ellen said. "Are you coming to bed, Lila?"

"In a second," Lila said, as she was laying out a pair of jeans and a T-shirt on top of the dresser.

"Why are you getting out clothes?" Jessica asked.

"For tomorrow," Lila answered quickly. "I like to be prepared."

When everyone was in bed, Jessica flicked off the light. " 'Night, you guys," she said, pretending to yawn.

She reached under her blanket, where she had hidden the candle that she had bought earlier, a book of matches from the floating restaurant, a rubber band, and Kenji's recipe. She waited for several tense minutes until Lila and Ellen were breathing evenly.

Then she pulled her hair into a ponytail on top of her head and gathered up her supplies. Quietly, she eased out of bed and tiptoed to the bathroom to await the stroke of midnight.

# Seventeen

◇

Lila opened her eyes and waited for them to adjust to the dark.

"Ellen?" she whispered. "Jessica?"

Steady breathing was her only answer.

Carefully, Lila got out of bed. She dressed in the clothes she had left on the dresser, then reached into her open suitcase and pulled out the envelope she had hidden there.

*To Whom It May Concern*, read the envelope. Inside was the farewell letter she had written after returning to the hotel that evening. She had locked herself in the bathroom while she wrote it, then smuggled it out in the pocket of her robe.

She placed the envelope on her pillow, then tiptoed to the door. In the darkness she thought she could just make out Jessica's sleeping form burrowed under the covers.

Lila paused. She realized she didn't have any makeup with her. And she really did want to look her best meeting royalty, even if it was a dead king.

Lila tiptoed toward the bathroom, where she had left her cosmetics bag. The door was closed, and she noticed a tiny line of light seeping out from under it.

*That's strange,* she thought as she eased open the door. *Maybe someone left the light on.*

*"Stop!"* a voice cried, as Lila tripped over a stooped form.

"Who are you?" Lila screamed.

"What's going on?" Ellen called, throwing back the covers and leaping from bed.

"Jessica, is that you?" Lila demanded. "What are you *doing*?"

"And what have you done to your hair?" Ellen asked, poking her head in the door.

Suddenly, the room was flooded with light. "What's going on in here?" Mary asked crossly, as Mandy and Janet followed her in.

"Jessica's playing with matches," Lila reported.

"And experimenting with her hair," Ellen added.

"How come *you're* dressed?" Jessica said to Lila.

"I think *I* know," Mandy called, waving Lila's farewell letter in the air. "Lila was sneaking off to see a dead king!"

"Not another tour!" Ellen groaned.

"No, Ellen," Lila said irritably. "And it's a king's *tomb*, Mandy." She rushed over and grabbed her letter. Jessica blew out her candle and followed Lila into the bedroom.

"Could we please get to the bottom of this?" Mary demanded. "What's going on with you two?"

Lila sighed. "It's hard to know where to begin," she said, dropping onto the edge of her bed.

"How about the beginning?" Mandy suggested.

Lila held out her hand so everyone could see her ring. "This," she said sadly, "is the source of all my problems. I found it on the beach when we first got here, and it turns out it's the sacred burial ring of a Hawaiian king."

Mandy opened her mouth to speak, but Lila pressed on. "Anyway, ever since it's been on my finger, I've had bad luck. That's why I was going to the king's tomb, to return the ring. It's the only way I can break the curse."

"Why don't you just take it off?" Mary asked practically.

"It's impossible," Lila said. "It will only come off when I visit the tomb."

"Lila," Mandy interjected, "I hate to break it to you, but I have a ring just like that one. I bought it at a souvenir shop." She ran to her room and returned a moment later with a ring that was an exact duplicate of Lila's.

Lila shook her head sadly. "That's just a reproduction, Mandy. I'm wearing the original."

Mandy laughed. "I'll bet you anything that ring cost two dollars and fifty-nine cents, just like mine did."

Mary headed for the bathroom and came out with a bottle of sunscreen. "Here," she said. "Try putting some of this on your finger, Lila."

"It won't work," Lila warned, but she let Mary drizzle the oil on her finger.

Mary pulled, and the ring refused to budge. "See?" Lila said. "It's the curse—"

Before she could finish her sentence, the ring slipped off her finger into Mary's hand.

"It's a miracle!" Lila cried.

Mary peered inside the ring. "Aloha Souvenir Shop," she read.

"Let me see that!" Lila demanded, grabbing the ring. "It *does* say that! I can't believe it," Lila groaned. "If I ever get hold of that Kenji—"

"Did you say *Kenji*?" Jessica interrupted.

Lila nodded. "You've met him, too?"

"Does he have a friend with big dimples?"

"Lono," Lila said.

Jessica rolled her eyes. "He gave me this," she said, tossing the recipe on the bed. "It's supposed to remove the curse that's on me."

"And why are *you* cursed?" Mary asked skeptically. "Another ring?"

Jessica shook her head. She glanced over at the dresser, where her Pineapple People pin lay. "I, uh, . . . I sort of lied."

"And?" Mary pressed.

"Well, the Hawaiian gods get really annoyed with liars. At least, that's what Kenji told me."

"What lie did you tell?" Ellen asked.

Jessica could feel her cheeks flush. "You know my Poisonous Potato Salad?" she said. "It didn't really win the contest."

"We think the Pineapple People made a mistake," Mandy added.

"So *that's* why they kept calling you 'Miss Wakely'!" Lila exclaimed. "I *thought* that was weird."

"I know I should have told them about their mistake," Jessica said quickly, "but we were having such a good time, and I hated to ruin everyone's fun. I was afraid they'd send us home." She took a deep breath. "Anyway, this Kenji guy told me I could make it up to the gods if I followed an ancient recipe at midnight. I was supposed to mix up a potion by candlelight, then drink it."

Mandy giggled. "And you *believed* him?"

Jessica shrugged. "I was desperate. After that chair incident at dinner, I was willing to try anything."

"Let me see that recipe," Mary said, reaching for the folded piece of paper. She read it carefully, then sighed. "Jessica! This 'ancient' recipe calls for diet soda!"

"So?"

"So I don't think the ancient Hawaiians consumed a whole lot of diet drinks," Mary said with a laugh.

"Face it, Jess," Lila said. "We've both been had."

"All *three* of us have been had," Janet said quietly. "Kenji's the one who told me I was Princess Keiko."

Mandy giggled. "We tried to tell you that story was crazy, Janet."

Janet sighed. "I know. But he and Lono were so *convincing*. I mean, they bowed and everything."

Jessica clenched her fists. "I'm going to strangle those obnoxious guys! How dare they treat us like this!"

"Tomorrow morning," Lila said, "let's find them on the beach, and—and—"

"And what?" Jessica asked.

Lila threw up her hands. "*I* don't know!"

"Wait a minute," Mandy advised. "This calls for a plan, and a good one at that. You need to give these guys a taste of their own medicine." Mandy frowned thoughtfully. "What we need to do," she said slowly, "is force Kenji and Lono to apologize."

"Mandy's right. We'll have to scare them into it," Lila said. "They won't do it voluntarily."

"But how?" Ellen asked.

"Pele!" Janet answered instantly. "There's a threat nobody can top! When she gets riled up, she covers the islands in lava. If Kenji and Lono thought Pele was angry with them, they'd apologize in a flash!"

"Perfect, Janet!" Mary exclaimed. "Let's make Pele appear to the guys in person!"

"We'll need someone to play the part of Pele," Mandy said.

Jessica smiled. "Well, all right—" she began.

"No, not you, Jessica." Mandy shook her head. "The boys know you. As the only other actress here, I'm the logical choice, but there's a good chance they've seen me with you."

"How about Bambi?" Jessica suggested. "She's an actress."

"No way!" Lila protested.

"But she'd be perfect, Lila," Mandy argued, "and I'm sure she'd help us out—"

"*No,*" Lila insisted. "We'll just have to think of some other way."

"All right," Mandy agreed. "Look, I'm tired. Why don't we all sleep on it?"

"One thing's for sure," Jessica said forcefully. "We're going to make Kenji and Lono wish they'd never messed with the Unicorns!"

"By the way, Jess," Ellen said as she crawled back into bed. "Dump the new hair style. It just isn't you!"

"I still say there's got to be a way to get even with those guys," Lila said the next morning as everyone was getting dressed.

"Let's talk about it at breakfast," Jessica responded, heading for the door. "I'm starving!"

"Is everybody ready to eat?" Mandy asked.

"*I* am," Jessica said. "Hurry up, you guys!"

"I can't find my other sandal!" Ellen called. "Just give me a second!"

Jessica and Mandy stood in the hallway waiting for the rest of the Unicorns to join them. "I wonder if we should invite Bambi," Jessica said. She stepped closer to her door. "Today's her last day here in Hawaii."

"No way," Mandy warned. "Lila would kill you."

"Sh!" Jessica hissed. "I hear voices, Mandy!" Jessica placed her ear against the door to Bambi's room. "Mr. Fowler's in there, I think. Wait! He just said something about marriage!"

Mandy pressed her ear to the door, too. "Their voices are too muffled," she said. "I'm going to get a water glass. That's what they always do in the movies."

Mandy returned with the glass just as the rest of the group filed into the hallway. "What's going on?" Mary asked.

"Quiet!" Jessica commanded. "They're talking about marriage in there!"

"Give me that glass!" Lila said, grabbing it from Mandy's hand. She placed it against the door and pressed her ear to it. The others gathered around, pushing and shoving for position.

"Hey, there's no room for me!" Ellen complained.

"Climb on top of Jessica," Mandy suggested.

Jessica, who was on her hands and knees, was too busy listening to complain as Ellen climbed onto her back.

"He said, 'My daughter means the world to me,' " Lila reported.

"*Oh*," Ellen said with relief. "I thought he said 'My daughter's beans are curled for free'!"

"Quiet, Ellen!" Lila instructed. "There's more! He just said, 'If you want to marry me, then you must be a mother to my child'!"

"What did she say?" Mary whispered.

Lila adjusted her water glass. "She's afraid she's not ready for motherhood," she said in a low voice. "And that she'd be a lousy mom." Lila nodded. "She's got that right!"

Mary nudged Mandy. "Move over, will you?" she whispered. "I'm missing all the juicy stuff."

"Would you mind getting off my back before I'm crushed?" Jessica growled at Ellen.

"Everybody, quiet!" Lila instructed. "I can't hear anything!" She squinted in concentration, but the room was suddenly silent. "That's strange," she murmured. "They stopped—"

Just then the door flew open and the girls piled into the room. Lila landed on top of the heap, the water glass still in her hand.

"Well, well," Mr. Fowler said, his arms crossed over his chest. "Is this some new kind of tumbling routine?'' He took the glass from Lila's hand. "Needs work, girls," he said. "Definitely needs work."

"We were just—uh, heading down for breakfast," Jessica mumbled.

"Not anymore you're not," Mr. Fowler replied. "I think it's time we had a little talk."

# *Eighteen*

◈

"There's nothing to talk about!" Lila cried, struggling to her feet. "No matter what you say, I'll never call her *Mom!*"

Mr. Fowler frowned. "I should hope not," he said reasonably. "Her name is Bambi."

"How could you *do* this to me?" Lila wailed. "Everything was fine just the way it was! I *like* our life!" She stomped over to Bambi, who was sitting on the edge of the bed, her mouth half-open in surprise.

"You're absolutely right, you know!" Lila cried. "You'd make a *lousy* mother. To begin with, you—you . . . wear too much eye makeup for a mother! And no mother of mine would have such crummy taste in jewelry—"

"Lila," Jessica interrupted, "maybe you should calm down a little."

"That's easy for *you* to say!" Lila retorted,

whirling around to face her friends. "You're not about to become a stepdaughter!"

"Whoa!" Mr. Fowler said. He walked over to Lila and put his arm around her shoulder. "Sit down, Lila," he said firmly. "You, too, girls."

"George," Bambi said, "I think I know what's going on here."

Mr. Fowler nodded. "The script." He walked over to the night stand and picked up a thick sheaf of paper bound in a blue cover. "You girls weren't by any chance listening at the door just now, were you?"

Mandy gulped. "We may have overheard a word or two as we were passing by—"

"Uh huh. Those *words* you heard were from Bambi's script. I was helping her work through her part for the audition tomorrow."

Lila looked carefully at her father. Was he telling the truth? He had never lied to her before, but this story was awfully hard to believe.

"I'm auditioning for the part of Flame, the small-town girl who falls in love with Caleb Dakota," Bambi explained. "He's a rich widower with—"

"With a teenaged daughter!" Jessica finished. "You're talking about *Days of Turmoil*, aren't you, Bambi?"

"Why didn't you *say* so?" Janet cried. "We *love* that soap opera!"

Bambi shrugged. "I didn't want to make a big

deal out of it," she said quietly. "I probably won't get the part."

"You see what happens when you eavesdrop, Lila?" Mr. Fowler said.

"But the ring you gave her!" Lila protested. "Wasn't that an engagement ring?"

Bambi laughed. "Didn't you see that I was wearing it on my right hand?" she asked. "Besides," she added with a grin, "if I ever *do* get engaged someday, Lila, I'm going to insist on a diamond!"

Lila shook her head, still unconvinced. "But they heard you talking about motherhood in the restaurant!" she said, pointing to Mandy and Mary. "And you told someone named Sid you hoped you'd be a beautiful bride!"

"How—" Bambi began. Then she shook her head and laughed. "Oh, well," she said, "when I was your age, I was pretty sneaky, too! Sid is my agent, Lila. And all the talk about motherhood and marriage had to do with the part."

Lila sniffed. She wasn't sure *what* to believe now.

Bambi looked at Mr. Fowler. "George," she said softly, "do you think Lila and I could have a moment alone?"

"Of course," he said. He took Lila's hand and gave it a squeeze. "Just remember one thing, honey," he whispered. "*I* like our life, too, just the way it is."

"You do, Daddy?" Lila asked.

"Absolutely."

Mr. Fowler headed for the door and held it open. "Well?" he said. "Come on, Unicorns! What are you waiting for? Let's go get ourselves some breakfast!"

When everyone had left, Lila got up from the bed. She felt abandoned, all alone with Bambi in her room. She had said some pretty rotten things to her. There was no telling how Bambi was going to retaliate.

"You know, Lila," Bambi began, "I think I understand what you're going through."

"How could you possibly understand?" Lila asked defensively.

"Well, my mom died when I was ten," Bambi explained quietly. "I was the oldest kid in my family, and I took over a lot of the responsibilities."

"That must have been tough," Lila conceded.

Bambi nodded. "It was. But after a long time, we all got settled in our new routine, my dad and my two brothers and I. My life was different from that of my other friends, but it was OK, you know? We made it work. We were happy. And I wouldn't have wanted anyone to suddenly come along and change that."

Lila sniffed again. She hated to admit it, but Bambi *did* understand.

"Anyway," Bambi said quickly, "I just want you to know that I don't want to change your life or become your stepmom. Although if I ever *do* have a daughter, I'd be proud to have one just like you. Maybe I've been pushing a little too hard, but I was only hoping that you and I could become friends. I'm really not so bad, once you get to know me."

"Me, either," Lila said, managing a smile.

Bambi laughed, and a single tear rolled down her cheek, leaving a dark trail of mascara in its wake.

Lila cleared her throat. "Honestly, Bambi!" she said, dashing to the bathroom for a tissue. "Haven't you heard of waterproof mascara? How are you ever going to play the part of Flame? The characters on *Days of Turmoil* cry constantly!"

Lila sat back down on the bed next to Bambi and handed her the tissue. "You know," she said quietly, "I didn't really mean what I said about your eye makeup."

Bambi draped an arm around Lila's shoulder as she wiped away her tear. "I know," she said, smiling. "But you *did* mean what you said about my crummy taste in jewelry, didn't you?"

"Well, yes," Lila admitted. "But if you hang around me long enough, I'm sure some of my good taste will rub off!"

"You know, when I suggested we go shopping after breakfast, this wasn't exactly what I had in mind, girls!" Bambi exclaimed as she and the Unicorns walked past a long row of souvenir shops.

"I'm so glad you've decided to help us out, Bambi!" Mandy said excitedly.

"I'm still not sure I can pull off this role, but I'm

willing to give it a try!" Bambi said. "Just remember that my plane leaves at nine this evening."

"You'll have plenty of time," Lila assured her. "We'll help you pack this afternoon."

"Let's see." Bambi surveyed the packages the Unicorns were carrying. "We've already got the fluorescent face paint and the black light. We're making real progress. Just a few more stops, and we'll be finished!"

"The paint is a great idea!" Jessica said.

"Yeah, it is. I learned about it in acting class," Bambi replied. "All those years of study came in handy, after all."

The group turned the corner and spotted Mr. Fowler waiting patiently in his rental car in a parking lot across the street.

"I just can't believe we know a soap opera star," Jessica marveled for the hundredth time since breakfast.

"Now don't go jumping the gun, Jessica," Bambi warned. "The competition for this role is going to be fierce. I was lucky just to get an audition." She sighed wistfully. "I'm sure I won't get the part, but at least the audition will be good experience."

"Bambi, you've got to think positively!" Lila exclaimed.

"I just *know* you're going to get the role," Mandy added.

"Thanks, guys," Bambi said. "But I *never* get the role."

"What are you all up to?" Mr. Fowler asked as the group approached the car.

"Girl stuff," Bambi replied.

"I'll be right back!" Lila said suddenly. "I want to check out that store we passed a minute ago."

"You mean that tacky little jewelry store?" Jessica said. "They would't have anything you'd want, Lila. Trust me."

"Probably not," Lila agreed. "But there was something in the window that caught my eye. I'll be back in a second."

The rest of the group crowded into the car. A few minutes later, Lila returned from the jewelry store. "You were right," she told Jessica. "It was a waste of time."

"Where to next?" Mr. Fowler asked as he pulled out of the parking lot.

Bambi turned around and smiled at the Unicorns. "Why, the grass skirt store, of course!"

"I hope you know what you're getting yourself into," Mr. Fowler warned Bambi with a smile.

"Of course I do," Bambi replied confidently. "The role of a lifetime!"

The sun had begun to sink when Janet set out on her mission. She walked along the nearly empty beach, her heart pounding loudly in her chest. She knew that Kenji and Lono could usually be found on the beach until dark, but there was no sign of them now, and the area was now almost deserted.

Janet paused to admire the brilliant sunset. *What if I can't pull this off?* she wondered anxiously. Jessica and Mandy were the actors in the group. Once again, she wished she had had more time to practice her lines.

"Princess Keiko? Is that you?"

Janet spun around to see Kenji and Lono behind her, bowing. "You may rise," she said regally.

The boys straightened, and together the three continued to walk along the beach.

"I see you've taken our advice," Kenji said.

"Advice?" Janet echoed.

"About staying in Hawaii."

Janet stopped walking. "Actually, I've decided to leave Hawaii after all."

Kenji gasped. "But you *can't!*" he cried. "We'll all be killed. Pele will—"

"Yes, yes, I know," Janet said, waving her hand impatiently. "But I checked it out with Pele." Janet paused for effect. "And she said it was OK for me to leave."

Kenji looked over at Lono uneasily. "What do you mean you checked it out with Pele?"

"I conjured her. You know, raised her spirit," Janet said matter-of-factly. "We princesses have special powers, you know?"

"No," Lono said. "That's not possible!"

"Why not?"

"Because"—Lono shot a glance at Kenji—"because she doesn't talk to just anybody."

"But I'm not just *anybody*," Janet pointed out. "I'm Princess Keiko."

"Yes, but—"

"Do you doubt me?"

"It's not doubt, exactly, Princess," Kenji said. "It's just that Pele's not supposed to be very—well, talkative."

Janet crossed her arms over her chest. "You dare to challenge the word of Princess Keiko?"

"Well—" Kenji began.

"Silence!" Janet commanded. "Follow me, and you will see Pele for yourself!"

Kenji and Lono exchanged looks. "You're going to take us to see her?" Kenji asked incredulously.

"Of course."

"*This* I gotta see," Lono whispered to Kenji.

*Me too*, Janet thought, as she led the way down the deserted beach.

# *Nineteen*

◇

"Where are you taking us?" Lono asked as Janet walked briskly along the edge of the water.

She thought he sounded just a little anxious. *So far, so good.* "To Pele, of course," she replied.

"You mean she hangs out on the beach?" Kenji asked. Janet noted that his eyes were darting back and forth nervously.

"She can appear as she wills," Janet replied.

She looked ahead to the little grove of palm trees the Unicorns had visited earlier that day with Bambi. It was nearly dark now, and there was no way for Janet to tell if everyone was in place. She would just have to hope for the best.

"Quiet now," Janet said, closing her eyes. "I'm trying to communicate with her."

Up ahead, Janet could make out the swaying forms of the palm trees and the outline of the brick-lined area where luaus—traditional Hawaiian feasts—were held.

"That's the luau pit up there," Lono said. "Maybe Pele's having a luau!"

Janet spun around, her hands on her hips. "I told you to be quiet!" she said haughtily.

"Look," Kenji said, taking a step backward, "this is really crazy. I'm going to head on home. Are you coming, Lono?"

"*Silence!*"

Janet gasped and spun on her heel in the sand. The voice was so loud and unexpected that even she was frightened.

There in the luau pit stood Bambi—only she didn't look at all like Bambi anymore. She was wearing a grass skirt and bikini top, and layers of beads around her neck that rattled as she moved. Kenji and Lono looked at her, their faces frozen in fear.

"Pele!" Kenji whispered.

"She's glowing!" Lono moaned.

Bambi had carefully painted her face, arms, and legs with several colors of fluorescent paint. Under the eerie blue glow of the black light they had inserted in one of the hanging lamps over the luau pit that afternoon, Bambi looked like a warrior painted for battle.

Bambi took a step forward. "Are these the boys Kenji and Lono?" she demanded in a voice so deep, Janet found it hard to believe it belonged to Bambi.

"Yes, Pele," Janet answered. She glanced over

at the bushes where she knew the Unicorns were hiding, but there was no sign of the girls.

"Step forth!" Bambi commanded.

"Y-you mean us?" Lono stammered.

"Now!"

Lono and Kenji took a few tentative steps forward.

"You have angered the goddess Pele," Bambi said. "Do you know why?"

Kenji shook his head. "No, ma'am," he said in a quavering voice. "I mean, Your Highness. I mean, Your Goddess—"

"Silence!" Bambi commanded again. "I will give you one more chance to answer my question." She took another step closer. The new moon suddenly peeked out from behind a cloud, and the combination of black light and moonlight made her painted face glow even more eerily. "Tell me how you have been treating the good visitors to my homeland!"

Kenji swallowed nervously. "Well, I, uh, we—we've been teasing them a little bit, maybe, but we didn't mean any harm by it, Pele—"

"Silence, fool! This is my home! How dare you refuse visitors the welcome they deserve!"

"It was just a little joke," Lono said meekly.

"Pele has no sense of humor!" Bambi boomed.

Janet covered her mouth with her hand to hide her smile. Bambi was definitely getting into her role.

"You leave me no choice!" Bambi cried. "To punish your transgressions, I must punish all the island!"

"No!" Kenji protested frantically. "Not that!"

"Maui must be buried in lava!"

"No!" Lono cried. "We're sorry, Pele! Really we are!"

"Sorry?" Bambi repeated. "Sorry?'

"Yes!" Kenji swore as he dropped to his knees. "Yes!"

Bambi shrugged. "Then tell it to them!" she said in her normal voice, pointing to the bushes.

The Unicorns emerged from their hiding places and surrounded the two boys.

Kenji stared at Bambi in disbelief. "But you glow!" he said.

"Fluorescent paint, Kenji," Janet explained.

"You *tricked* us!" Lono cried.

"How dare you!" Kenji protested.

"How dare *us*?" Lila demanded. "What about you guys, with my sacred ring, and Jessica's 'ancient' recipe? Not to mention Princess Keiko over there," she said, nodding toward Janet.

"Just what was the big idea, anyway?" Jessica asked.

Kenji smiled sheepishly. "OK. I guess we got out of hand."

"See, most of the guys we hang around with do two things all day," Lono explained. "Surf, and make fun of tourists. Kenji and I actually talk to tourists—you know, give them directions, that kind of thing."

"So?" Jessica demanded. "How come you were picking on us, then?"

"At first we thought that if we gave you a hard time, our friends would stop making fun of us for being nice to tourists."

"So there never really was a Princess Keiko?" Janet asked.

Kenji shook his head. "We just made her up. But some of the things we told you were true. There really was a King Kamehameha, for example. And remember that Hawaiian saying I told you about, Jessica—'The Life of the Land is Perpetuated in Righteousness'? That's really the Hawaiian state motto." Kenji grinned. "I guess once we got started telling stories, we just couldn't stop!"

"Besides," Lono added, "it gave us a chance to talk to beautiful California girls!"

"So, if you're not too mad at us, maybe you'd all like to come to a New Year's Eve luau here on the beach tomorrow night," Kenji said shyly. "We'll understand if you don't want to."

"I don't know. Lila, what do you think?" Jessica asked.

Lila grinned. "Ask the Princess!"

"I'll have to check my royal calendar," Janet answered regally, "but I think we can fit you in!"

"Great!" Kenji looked at Bambi again. "You

sure had me fooled," he said. "I was scared to death!"

"Me, too," Lono agreed.

Bambi shrugged. "Well, the makeup helped."

"No, it wasn't the makeup as much as the way you acted," Kenji said. "You ought to go into acting, lady!"

Bambi laughed, too. "You know," she said, "maybe I will!"


"Be sure to call us and let us know how the audition went!" Mr. Fowler said as Bambi prepared to board her plane later that evening.

The Unicorns crowded around her in the airport waiting area. "I will," Bambi said. "You know, after my acting debut as Pele, I'm feeling more confident about this audition."

"Go get 'em!" Jessica said.

"We'll be rooting for you!" Ellen added.

Bambi smiled at all the girls. "I want to thank you all," she said.

"For what?" Mandy asked.

"For helping to prepare me for the role of Flame. I've learned a lot more than I ever really wanted to know about motherhood, thanks to you girls!"

"This is your last call to board Flight 1687 to Los Angeles!" came a voice over the loudspeaker.

"That's me!" Bambi said. She gave Mr. Fowler a kiss, then hugged each of the girls.

Everyone waved as Bambi got in line to board her plane.

"Oh, no!" Lila cried. "I almost forgot!" She ran over to Bambi and joined her in line. "Look, Bambi!" she said excitedly, holding out her wrist. "I forgot to tell you that I found the charm bracelet this afternoon! It was in my cosmetics case all the time!"

"No kidding!" Bambi leaned close and examined the bracelet. Then she broke into a smile. "Your cosmetics case, huh?"

Lila nodded.

"Then I wonder how the bracelet managed to grow three extra heart charms?" Bambi asked.

"Uh-oh," Lila said.

"You bought another bracelet while we were shopping today, didn't you?" Bambi asked. "I *wondered* why you insisted on going back to that tacky jewelry shop!"

Lila nodded. She had thought she was being so clever, and now Bambi was going to think she was a complete fool.

"That's one of the sweetest things anyone's ever done for me, Lila," Bambi asked. "I know you hated that bracelet."

"Not anymore," Lila said sincerely.

"Tell you what. Next time I'm in Sweet Valley, let's you and I go shopping together and see if a little of your good taste in jewelry can rub off on me. Who knows? I may be a rich and famous actress by then!'' She reached over and gave Lila another hug.

"It's a deal,'' Lila agreed. "And Bambi?''

"Yes?''

"Break a leg!''

# *Twenty*

◈

"I still say we shouldn't be wasting *another* day of our vacation with the Pineapple People!" Lila complained Monday morning.

Jessica paused in front of the doors to the company lobby. "I have to get this off my chest, Lila," she said firmly. "I'm tired of feeling guilty."

"Me, too," Mandy agreed.

Jessica entered the lobby and led the Unicorns to the receptionist's desk. "I'd like to see Mr. Hakulani," she said nervously.

"Do you have an appointment?"

"Well, no. But it's very important. Tell him it's Jessica Wakefield—uh, Wakely."

"Well, which is it?" the receptionist asked.

"Wakely," Mandy answered quickly.

A few minutes later, the receptionist led the girls to Mr. Hakulani's large modern office. Pictures of pineapples hung on the walls, and a brass sculpture of a pineapple sat on his desk.

"Miss Wakely!" he said happily. "Come in and have a seat. And to what do I owe this great honor? No problems with your vacation, I hope?"

"Just one," Jessica answered. She swallowed hard. Somehow this had seemed like a better idea back at the hotel. "I'm not the real winner of the contest, Mr. Hakulani," she blurted out. "There's been a terrible mistake."

"Mistake? What kind of mistake?"

Jessica took a deep breath. "My name is really Jessica Wakefield. And for your cooking contest I entered a really horrible pineapple recipe, with green food coloring—"

"And anchovies," Mandy added.

Mr. Hakulani curled his lip in distaste. "It certainly does sound terrible!"

"But I wanted to believe I'd won. I mean, my brother Steven ate my green glop, so I figured maybe it wasn't so bad."

"Of course, Steven'll eat *anything*," Mandy interrupted.

"I see," Mr. Hakulani said.

Jessica nodded. "When I got here, and you started calling me Jessica *Wakely*, I knew something was wrong, but by then, we were having such a good time—" Jessica paused. "So you see my point."

Mr. Hakulani reached over to a pile of folders on his desk and shuffled through them. "Here it is," he said. "The contest file." For a few minutes he read the contents of the file in silence. "Aha!" he said finally.

"Aha?" Jessica asked.

"Here's where the problem came in," he said. "Someone typed a memo incorrectly. They typed *Wakely* instead of *Wakefield*."

Jessica shook her head. She did not see. "You mean I *did* win?"

Mr. Hakulani nodded. "Of course."

"But the pineapple upside-down cake?"

"Our own recipe." Mr Hakulani grinned. "You see, Jessica, all the recipes we received were, quite honestly, disgusting. So we decided, just for the fun of it, to award the prize to the *worst* recipe instead of the best. Yours was the clear winner."

Lila giggled. "She *is* a lousy cook," she agreed.

Jessica felt as if a weight had been lifted from her shoulders. "You mean there never was a Jessica Wakely?"

"No."

"And my green glop *did* win?"

"Yes, in a manner of speaking."

Jessica let out a deep sigh of relief.

"And for your admirable honesty," Mr. Hakulani said, "I'm going to reward you with two hundred cans of the Pineapple People Company's finest crushed pineapple!"

"But that's not necessary, really," Jessica said quickly.

"Nonsense. I insist," Mr. Hakulani said as he

ushered the girls out the door. "We'll mail them right to your house in California."

"See what honesty gets you, Jess?" Lila said when they had returned to the lobby.

"Yeah," she sighed. "A lifetime's supply of pineapple."

Elizabeth was going to be *so* excited.

"Elizabeth says happy new year to everybody!" Jessica said that evening as she set down the phone.

"How'd she take the pineapple news?" Lila asked.

"She was thrilled," Jessica said with a laugh.

"Is everybody ready?" Mandy asked. "Kenji said the luau starts around eight."

"Let's go!" Ellen said. "I'm starving!"

The Unicorns were almost out the door when the phone rang. "I'll get it," Lila said, dashing back. "Hello?" she said into the phone.

"I have a person-to-person call to Lila from Flame," said an operator.

"Flame?" Lila repeated. "I don't know any— oh, yes, I do!" she cried. "Hey, everybody, come quick! I think it's Bambi!"

"Lila?" Bambi said, her voice dim on the crackling line. "I got the part! I'm going to be a stepmother after all!"

"She did it!" Lila shouted, as the group began to cheer. Lila held up the phone so Bambi could hear them yelling.

"I think I gained some extra confidence after playing the demanding part of Pele," Bambi said.

"We *knew* you could do it!" Lila exclaimed.

"Tell your dad I said hi," Bambi added. "I just wanted you to be the first to know!"

"Thanks," Lila said. "And you know what, Bambi? I think you're going to make a great stepmom!"

"Meka, I want you to meet Jessica, Lila, Janet, and Ellen," Kenji said that night at the luau. A large crowd had gathered to welcome in the new year.

"Are these the tourists you've been telling stories to?" asked Meka, a tall, dark-haired boy.

"Has he ever!" Jessica smiled at Kenji. "But don't worry! We got even!"

"So I heard," said Meka. "As far as I'm concerned, tourists who are *this* pretty can have all the directions they want!"

Jessica excused herself and walked over to join Mandy and Mary, who were watching the flames flicker in the big fire at the center of the luau pit. "Kenji and Lono definitely have some nice friends," Jessica said.

"There *are* an awful lot of cute guys here," Mary said. She sighed wistfully. "I can't believe we really have to leave tomorrow. I wish we could stay forever. Or at least come back soon."

"Me, too." Mandy smiled. "Say, you don't have your wallet with you, do you, Jess?"

"No, why?"

Mandy stood. "Where's Mr. Fowler?" she asked.

Jessica pointed past the fire, where a girl was giving hula lessons. "He's doing the hula!" Jessica exclaimed.

"Come on," Mandy said. The girls walked over to Mr. Fowler, who was swaying back and forth with a group of men and women.

"You sure do a mean hula, Mr. Fowler," Jessica said.

"I'm not half bad, am I?" he said grinning. "For an old dad."

"Do you have three pennies we could borrow?" Mandy asked.

"Why, sure." Mr. Fowler stopped his hula long enough to reach into his pants pocket. "There you go."

"Thanks," Mandy said. She signaled to Mary and Jessica and headed down to the water's edge. "Here," she said, giving each girl one of the coins.

"What's this for?" Jessica asked.

Mandy closed her eyes and tossed the penny into the ocean. "Make a wish," she instructed.

"Here goes mine," Mary said.

Jessica smiled. She squeezed her eyes shut and threw her coin far out into the waves.

Somehow, she was sure they had all wished for the very same thing.

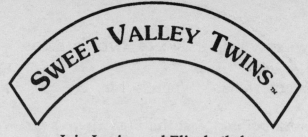

# SWEET VALLEY TWINS ™

| | | | |
|---|---|---|---|
| ☐ | 15681-0 | **TEAMWORK #27** | $2.75 |
| ☐ | 15688-8 | **APRIL FOOL! #28** | $2.75 |
| ☐ | 15695-0 | **JESSICA AND THE BRAT ATTACK #29** | $2.75 |
| ☐ | 15715-9 | **PRINCESS ELIZABETH #30** | $2.95 |
| ☐ | 15727-2 | **JESSICA'S BAD IDEA #31** | $2.75 |
| ☐ | 15747-7 | **JESSICA ON STAGE #32** | $2.99 |
| ☐ | 15753-1 | **ELIZABETH'S NEW HERO #33** | $2.99 |
| ☐ | 15766-3 | **JESSICA, THE ROCK STAR #34** | $2.99 |
| ☐ | 15772-8 | **AMY'S PEN PAL #35** | $2.95 |
| ☐ | 15778-7 | **MARY IS MISSING #36** | $2.99 |
| ☐ | 15779-5 | **THE WAR BETWEEN THE TWINS #37** | $2.99 |
| ☐ | 15789-2 | **LOIS STRIKES BACK #38** | $2.99 |
| ☐ | 15798-1 | **JESSICA AND THE MONEY MIX-UP #39** | $2.95 |
| ☐ | 15806-6 | **DANNY MEANS TROUBLE #40** | $2.99 |
| ☐ | 15810-4 | **THE TWINS GET CAUGHT #41** | $2.99 |
| ☐ | 15824-4 | **JESSICA'S SECRET #42** | $2.95 |
| ☐ | 15835-X | **ELIZABETH'S FIRST KISS #43** | $2.95 |
| ☐ | 15837-6 | **AMY MOVES IN #44** | $2.95 |
| ☐ | 15843-0 | **LUCY TAKES THE REINS #45** | $2.99 |
| ☐ | 15849-X | **MADEMOISELLE JESSICA #46** | $2.95 |
| ☐ | 15869-4 | **JESSICA'S NEW LOOK #47** | $2.95 |
| ☐ | 15880-5 | **MANDY MILLER FIGHTS BACK #48** | $2.99 |
| ☐ | 15899-6 | **THE TWINS' LITTLE SISTER #49** | $2.99 |
| ☐ | 15911-9 | **JESSICA AND THE SECRET STAR #50** | $2.99 |

**Bantam Books, Dept. SVT5, 414 East Golf Road, Des Plaines, IL 60016**

Please send me the items I have checked above.  I am enclosing $_____
(please add $2.50 to cover postage and handling).  Send check or money
order, no cash or C.O.D.s please.

Mr/Ms _____

Address _____

City/State _____ Zip _____

SVT5-9/91

Please allow four to six weeks for delivery.
Prices and availability subject to change without notice.